Transport
Death Mission

Phillip P. Peterson

1. An Unexpected Visit

"Up! Hands through the hatch."

Russell Harris needed a moment to rouse himself from his dark thoughts and squinted in confusion at the slit in the steel door. Usually the condemned were left in peace during their final days.

"What's up, Dan? Cell check?"

Harris stood up and dragged himself over to the heavy steel door. He put both his hands through the hatch. Dan, who had obviously taken over the shift from Walter, handcuffed him.

"No more checks, Harris. Visitor. Now stand back against the wall."

Russell shuffled backward until he felt the wall against his back. When Dan unlocked the cell door he placed his shackled hands on his stomach. The guard kneeled down in front of him and snapped more cuffs around his ankles. Russell looked up and saw Joe standing in the corridor staring sullenly into the cell.

Joe—full name Joseph Street—was the death row supervisor. At this time of day he was normally joking with his pals at his local bar about the next execution. If he was still in the prison at this hour it must be important.

Dan stood up again and Russell faced him like an unequal duelist. The guard then grabbed him by the handcuffs and pulled him out of the cell. Slowly they made their way down the corridor. The floor covering caused the soles of Russell's shoes to squeak as he walked. He hadn't expected any more visitors before his execution.

"Is it my lawyer? I thought he was on his way to

the Caribbean after the clemency appeal was rejected."

The very idea made Russell chuckle. His workaholic hack lawyer would never go on vacation of his own free will. After a day's work, he would more likely drop into his local hospital ER to convince the injured to hire him.

"It ain't your lawyer," grunted Joe.

He sensed that the guards were uneasy. Obviously his mysterious visitor had come up with some damn good arguments. He stopped in front of the door to the visitors' room, but Dan kept pulling him toward the exit of the death row unit. Russell felt himself resisting. He had already accepted that he would be leaving death row in the other direction—headed for the execution chamber and the electric chair.

The guard stepped forward and unlocked the steel door.

"Joe, I didn't expect to be walking through this door anymore."

They continued past the surveillance room where the officers usually sat. Then they went through the outer door. Straight ahead was the door to the main building with its windows of thick leaded glass. They turned right into a corridor that led to some offices and storerooms. Through the open door of a meeting room, a shaft of bright light fell across the floor. A man in a black suit was standing next to the door and staring vacantly at the opposite wall. A Secret Service agent, Russell concluded from the earpiece.

They stepped into the room, which wasn't very large; it was designed for meetings between the guards and prison management. Sometimes relatives of a death-row inmate waited here for the execution to begin. In the middle of the room was a round, worn wooden table, surrounded by some uncomfortable-looking chairs. The walls were yellowing and bare. A photo of President Bigby hung slightly askew below a shelf with a small plasma TV. On the far side of the table sat a man in a dark-blue uniform. The visitor turned his eyes to Russell. They were brown, almost black eyes that Russell hadn't seen in a long time. The two men looked at each other blankly.

"Sir, I still don't know what all this is about," Joe broke the silence.

The man at the table stood up, finally turned his gaze away from Russell and stared irritably at the guard.

"Lieutenant Street, you have the papers, which are signed by the President of the United States. You spoke on the phone with the Department of Justice and had the letter verified. If I have to wait any longer there could be hell to pay."

It was a voice that Russell hadn't heard in quite a while. A voice that had always instilled fear in him. Colonel Morrow never hesitated to act on his words, as Russell knew from personal experience.

"I'll have hell to pay when Senator Gould hears about this," said Joe in a whiny voice. "He was looking forward to watching this bastard go to hell next Tuesday!"

Russell could feel his pulse quickening. Was his execution being postponed? Was he going to be granted clemency? Normally the President never got involved in the judicial affairs of the individual states, but perhaps Bigby had intervened on his behalf. After all, it was he who had presented him with the medal for bravery. At the time, Russell had run about a mile through enemy fire in order to reach his injured comrades. That had not gone unnoticed by certain people. Was saving someone's life now enough for him to be pardoned? But clemency would mean *for life* —and what did Morrow have to do with it?

"That's your problem, Lieutenant. And now please remove this man's handcuffs."

"I can only do that after you've signed the amnesty declaration, General!"

General. Russell looked at the uniform's insignia. Of course. It had been obvious that Morrow would be promoted to general at some point. His political instinct was as infamous as his razor-sharp intellect. He wondered which unit Morrow was commanding now.

The general's face relaxed. He was well aware of the trouble the lieutenant was facing.

"Alright. Now please leave us alone. Agent Smith will call you when we're done."

With a grim expression on his face, Joe left the room and the agent locked the door on the outside. They were alone. The general walked around the table to Russell, until they were face to face.

"Good to see you, General. It's been a long time,"

"Yes, indeed, Soldier."

Russell chuckled softly. "I'm not a soldier anymore."

"You will be one again, Harris. If you accept my offer, you will be one again."

"You want to save me from death row and stick me back in the army?" He laughed again. "It must be a pretty ugly mission, Sir. It's unusual for the army to recruit death-row inmates."

"Sit down, Harris. It's complicated, because there's a lot that I'm not allowed to explain to you. At least not until you've made a decision."

Russell sat down and laid his shackled hands on the table. The general placed his hands on the back of Russell's chair and leaned over his shoulder.

"Listen to me, Harris. I don't want to give you any false hopes. I'm still with the army, but as the head of a special unit. I report directly to the President."

"What kind of a special ..."

Morrow raised a hand. "Let me finish talking, then you can ask your questions! It's not a combat mission, I can tell you that much."

Russell gave him a puzzled look.

"It's a fact-finding and reconnaissance mission. The chances of survival are slim, which is why the President is making the following offer: you take part in ten extremely dangerous missions and get the chance to sacrifice your life for your country, perhaps even for the good of all humanity. If you survive the ten missions, you will be granted amnesty. You are one of ten prisoners to be given this opportunity. Now you can ask your questions. But I won't be able to tell you much more. You have five minutes to decide."

Russell's head was spinning.

"Sir ... You want to take me out of here to deploy me in a secret mission in which I will undoubtedly die? What kind of mission has such a minimal chance of success? Do you want to send me into a volcano?"

"It's possible that you might emerge in a

volcano."

Russell frowned. "Where do you want to send me?"

"That's precisely what you need to find out."

"You don't know where you want to send me?"

The general nodded. "Correct, Harris. If you accept my offer, we will leave this prison together in one minute. You don't belong here anyway. Over the coming weeks, you'll find out more while you prepare for your mission."

"Why me of all people?"

"You took part in the Leo project. The training you received should pay off."

Harris swallowed. The Leo project was already some years back. The training had involved hand-to-hand combat in zero gravity. His unit had flown countless reduced-gravity flights in an old NASA vomit comet, because some big shot in the Pentagon had decided they should be prepared for the possibility of boarding the Chinese Tiangong space station, which was orbiting close to Earth. In an emergency, his team would have been put in an Orion capsule and sent up in a Delta rocket. After the new president was elected, the project had been buried as clandestinely as it had been brought to life.

But what has that got to do with this situation? Do they want to put me on a rocket and shoot me up into space?

Russell shook his head. There were astronauts and test pilots for that kind of thing. It must be something pretty awful for them to enlist death-row inmates.

But it's definitely better than kicking the bucket on the electric chair in a few days.

"I don't have much of a choice, do I?"

General Morrow looked him in the eye. "No, Harris, you don't. But I can tell you one thing: we don't either!"

The general signed the amnesty declaration and knocked on the door. Joe came into the room, swearing. He removed the shackles from Russell's feet, and then his handcuffs. They left the building through a back door and got into a black limousine. Agent Smith was at the wheel.

Nobody stopped them at the main entrance to the compound, either.

From prisoner and death-row inmate back to being a soldier ...

It was surreal. The legal machinery of the state moved incredibly slowly. Even a visit from his lawyer involved stacks of paperwork and it took days until the visit actually took place. In contrast, the switch from prisoner to soldier had taken less than 60 seconds.

As they sped along Highway 32, Russell squinted into the darkness outside.

"So what happens next?" he asked.

General Morrow had turned on his reading light and was rummaging through various papers.

"First stop is Cleveland Municipal Airport," he explained, while reading a document. "Two aircraft are waiting for us there. One for me and one for you. I'm flying to Florence to see the next candidate and you're flying to Nevada."

"To Nevada? Let me guess: if this project is so secretive and dangerous, I must be headed for Area 51."

Russell smiled to himself; he'd meant it as a joke.

"Not quite, but nearly. Yucca Flats."

"The former nuclear test site?" Russell asked in amazement. He hadn't reckoned with that. Suddenly his heart sunk: would he have to walk through the bomb craters so that scientists could study the effects of the radiation?

"I can see from your expression what you're thinking, Harris. But let me reassure you, the project has nothing to do with nuclear weapons. We can work in peace on the site and the residual radiation covers up our own emissions."

"What's it all about? Can't you give me any more concrete details?"

"No, not at the moment. You'll find out about the project and your mission soon enough. In Yucca you'll meet the other volunteers, and our instructors will get you back into shape." Morrow scanned him from head to toe. "It looks like you haven't exercised much lately."

"My cell was a little small to play football."

The general smiled. "You certainly haven't lost your sense of humor. Enjoy your few days of freedom. It will get unpleasant soon enough. Parallel to the physical training you will learn to use various pieces of equipment, then you'll find out the details of your mission. Your first transport will take place in four weeks."

"Transport? Transport to where, Sir?"

"Possibly straight to hell."

2. Flight to Nevada

At the airport there were two jets parked next to each other. Russell looked at the tails of the aircraft, and saw that they were both adorned with the Tepper Aviation logo. He knew this was a front for the CIA: the planes of the fictitious airline secretly flew alleged terrorists to interrogation facilities in Arab and Eastern European countries that were a little more lax when it came to human rights. Both cockpits were illuminated. A pilot was pacing between the two jets smoking a cigarette. When Morrow's car came to a halt in front of the aircraft, the pilot dropped the butt on the ground, crushed it with his heel and climbed the steps up to his jet. The general accompanied Russell to the door of the aircraft.

"Will we see each other in Nevada, General?"

"Only toward the end of your training. Make sure that you get back into shape. And another thing: We're not releasing any perverts or psychos from jail, but a few of the other candidates have got pretty dubious records. You're a good man and have leadership qualities. I'd appreciate your help in keeping the group under control. The president isn't too happy about the fact we're using jailbirds for this project, and I'll have to take the rap if the project gets out of control. And if it does, the whole group will be sent to a place where I can guarantee you won't survive. Keep that in mind, Harris!"

"Yes Sir," Russel replied. "One more thing ..."

"Yes, my son?"

"Thanks for getting me out of there."

"Don't thank me too soon. What awaits you might be worse than the electric chair!"

Russell gulped, but Morrow just laughed.

"It's okay, relax. You'll find a few cans of beer in the cooler at the back." The general nodded toward the cabin, and once Russell was inside he locked the door from the outside.

Russell noticed that their aircraft was gathering speed, and the pilot turned around in his seat to look at him.

"Take a seat and fasten your seatbelt. We've been cleared for takeoff and we're already taxiing. The flight time is about five hours."

Five hours from Mississippi to Nevada?

He hesitated, but decided not to ask.

The cabin was sparsely furnished. Six seats with two tables, behind that empty space.

Are those blood stains on the floor?

At the back of the cabin, behind a half-drawn curtain, he could make out a chemical toilet. He sat down in a window seat, reached into the cooler behind it and pulled out a can of beer. It was ice cold. He emptied it in one gulp, while the jet taxied along the runway and then took off.

Lost in thought, he gazed out of the window into the darkness. He mulled over what the general had told him, and wondered what it could all be about. At least he had escaped the electric chair, and no matter what dangers awaited him on this upcoming mission, surely they couldn't be worse than that.

After two hours, the aircraft suddenly plummeted, flew a wide curve close to the ground and then rose back up into the air.

"We need to make sure nobody follows our course."

Russell turned away from the window and looked

at the speaker. The pilot was standing in the doorway to the cockpit.

"We turned around under the radar and changed the transponder code," he explained. "Now we're taking the fastest route possible to Yucca Flats. We'll land shortly after sunrise."

The man tried to sound businesslike, but there was a hint of nervousness in his voice.

"What's bothering you?" asked Russell.

"Nothing. It's just a little unusual. Our passengers are usually are chained to the floor at the back when we chauffer them to Eastern Europe or Libya."

So I was right!

"I must be a special case."

The pilot shrugged, pulled out two bottles of water from the cooler and disappeared into the cockpit.

Many somber thoughts later, Russell saw rocky peaks and sand dunes bathed in the ghostly light of the moon. When the announcement came over the loudspeaker, the jet had already started its descent.

"Fasten your seat belt. We'll be landing in approximately fifteen minutes."

Russell did as he was told before turning to look out of the window again. Dawn was breaking, and below him in the pale light he could see a sand-colored lunar landscape dotted with craters. It seemed to him like he was flying over a scarred, weather-beaten face. He was looking at the remains of the many nuclear tests that the government had carried out in the desert decades ago.

The aircraft landed on a dusty concrete runway and ground to a halt. The door was immediately flung open and a brawny military policeman stormed in.

"Stand up! Out!" he bellowed and grabbed Russell by the shoulder.

"Take it easy."

"Don't tell me to take it easy! Get your ass out of this aircraft, you're not on vacation!"

The man hustled him down the stops where another military policeman was waiting next to an SUV. "Get in and keep your mouth shut! I don't want to hear a sound out of you!"

Russell sat down in the front passenger seat. The Jeep started with a jerk and headed into the desert.

It was a grueling drive. The brightness of the low sun stung his eyes and he could feel the heat on his skin, which was no longer used to sunlight.

After a few minutes, they turned onto a wide road that headed northward, across a dried-out salt lake and toward a distant mountain range. The landscape was randomly dotted with groups of buildings and tower-like structures rusting away in the blistering Nevada heat. At regular intervals Russell spotted flat, furrowed depressions in the sand. They looked like giant caves that had collapsed in on themselves and he guessed that these were craters produced by detonated atomic bombs.

"It's not a very hospitable landscape around here," he said to the driver of the Jeep.

The MP sitting in the back struck him on the head. "What did I say? You should shut the fuck up!" the man yelled in his ear.

Russell said no more, and folded his arms across his chest.

They drove for about twenty miles, until they reached a group of four buildings. The site was surrounded by high barbwire fences. They drove through a gate with a guard and came to a halt next to a run-down barrack.

"Get out."

Russell did as he was told. The soldier behind him took a firm hold of his arm and led him into the building. Several doors led off a corridor with wooden floorboards. They stopped outside the second-to-last door on the left.

The soldier opened it and thrust Russell inside. There was a rickety bed on the left-hand side of the cell. On the other side were a small table and a chair; a hole in the floor by the window served as a toilet. The soldier slammed the steel door shut and locked it.

Russell looked out of the window. He saw the fence and, beyond it, miles of sandy desert, which eventually merged into rocky mountains. Exhausted, he sat down on the bed and leant back against the wall. He closed his eyes and waited.

3. Training

Russell stayed in his cell for two days. A soldier brought him his meals on a plastic tray. He was given a combat uniform and a bag of toiletries. During this time he had nothing to do except lie on his bed and brood.

What have they got in store me? How am I going to die? It must be a mission deep into enemy territory with no chance of retreating!

On the morning of the third day, a soldier flung open the door and burst inside. "Get up! Get dressed and report outside the building in sixty seconds. Get a move on!"

Russell forced himself to be both composed and quick. Mechanically he pulled on his pants, but he almost collapsed from a head rush.

The soldier had meanwhile stomped off to the neighboring cell. He heard a crash on the other side of the wall. With trembling hands, Russell buttoned up his green-and-brown flecked shirt and pulled on the boots that he had already laced up the day before.

Suddenly the soldier was standing in the cell again.

"What did I say? You need to move your ass, before I kick you outside!"

Droplets of spittle sprayed in Russell's face. Without wiping them away, he hurried out of his cell and down the corridor, and bumped into a bald man who was rushing out of another cell. Together they stumbled outside. Some other men—and one woman—were standing in a disorderly line.

To the side, a gray-haired soldier with folded arms was standing guard and watching the spectacle with a grim expression.

"Move, move, in rank and file, you lazy shits! Line up in order of height and stand still!" yelled the man who came out of the building behind him.

Russell pushed himself between a man with a moustache and the woman, accidentally treading on her foot. He mumbled an apology but didn't get a reply.

Another prisoner stumbled out of the building and almost fell down the short flight of steps.

"In order of height, I said! You go here. No, here! What's your problem? Finally!"

The soldier stood in front of his superior, and saluted.

"All present and correct, Sergeant Niven!"

The sergeant nodded. Another soldier emerged from the barrack and grimaced.

"It stinks worse than a sewer in there! You'll have to clean up tonight!"

He went and stood next to his comrades. The sergeant stepped forward.

"Well, that's quite something," he said in irritated voice. "I've rarely been faced with such a pathetic, lousy-looking group." He shouted his way down the line and slapped one of the men around the head. "Look at me when I'm talking to you!"

The man opened his mouth to say something, but changed his mind at the last second.

"I have no idea why you fucking idiots were released from jail and if it was up to me I'd blow your brains out. But I've been ordered to turn you back into soldiers. And that's exactly what I'm going to do."

He stood in front of the group again and looked

the convicts in the eye, one by one. His upper lip trembled.

"You'll remember the next four weeks for the rest of your lives. And it won't be a good memory. You'll be begging me to send you back to jail. You'll run until you puke, and march until your feet are bloody lumps. Four weeks is nowhere near long enough to turn you bums back into human beings. If you think I feel even a glimmer of pity for you, then you are very much mistaken."

He started marching up and down the line again.

"I'm Sergeant Niven and this is Corporal Barnes and Corporal Gerrold. Whatever we tell you, it happens pronto, is that understood? Any funny business and I'll stick this club further up your ass than you ever thought possible!"

Russell didn't take this show seriously. He had seen it often enough during his years in the army. After being locked up for such a long time, he was in fact looking forward to some strenuous exercise and getting back into shape. He was far more worried about what awaited him after the four weeks of training were up. He also wondered about the others in his team. Some of them looked like they could be troublemakers—and he hadn't expected there to be a woman in the group.

He turned to look at her. She was a little smaller and younger than he was. Her alert eyes complemented her athletic body and even the combat uniform couldn't disguise the fact that she was very pretty.

Whack!

Sergeant Niven's hand landed on Russell's face.

"Eyes straight ahead, Soldier!"

As commanded, Russell looked to the front, even though his thoughts lingered on his comrade beside him. Well, they would get to know each other soon enough.

"Better already," said the sergeant. "And now everyone grab a backpack and move. On the double!" He pointed at a pile of backpacks off to the side. They appeared to be filled with something heavy, but nobody budged. He then glared at the group through narrowed eyes. "The person who gets the backpack marked with a red cross is on latrine duty tonight!"

Everyone dashed over to the pile. Russell had no trouble finding an unmarked backpack. When there were just two backpacks left, the woman ripped the one without the cross out of the hands of a much bigger prisoner. She squeezed the man's finger so hard that he cried out in pain.

Niven ran ahead and the group stumbled into a disorderly line behind him. Several feet beyond the gate to the compound, the sergeant stopped. "Halt! Not like that! Line up, one behind the other. You get behind me." He pointed at the tallest in the group. "Then in order of height. Better. And go! By lunch I want you to have completed twenty miles!"

Russell sprinted off with the rest of the group. They ran to the foot of the mountain, where the first prisoner collapsed. He vomited, although they had had no breakfast.

Corporal Barnes kicked him in the ribs. "You lazy piece of shit! Stand up and keep running!"

The man coughed, struggled to his feet and limped on.

They turned eastward and reached the edge of a wide trough, which must have once been a riverbed.

Running in the desert was exhausting. With every step they had to drag their feet out of the sand. Sand got into their heavy boots and rubbed the skin off their feet.

Russell got stomach cramps. He could feel the bile rising in his throat and had to vomit. He didn't bother to stop, but turned his head to the side and spat the burning stuff out. Years ago he had run a marathon in three-and-a-half hours, but he had been considerably fitter then and he hadn't been carrying a heavy backpack.

He looked around him. The woman was running behind him, bravely gritting her teeth. Her short blond hair was glistening with sweat.

Pretty tough, that one.

She reminded him of a medical officer who had been part of his unit in Afghanistan. They had hit if off immediately—but as a married man he had been careful not to overstep the mark. The medical officer had also been tough, and had never as much as winced during the long marches in the scorching heat at the Pakistan border. But her tenacity didn't help her any when she was hit by a piece of shrapnel and her brain was splattered across the wall of a house. From one moment to the next—a vibrant young woman turned into a heap of dead flesh.

He felt a tightness in his chest as he remembered the moment. During every patrol they had had to march past that goddamn house in that run-down shithole of a village. The walls were still stained red and yellow months later. A young sergeant who had also experienced the attack went ballistic one day and threw a hand grenade through a window of the building. Half of the façade caved in; fortunately nobody had been inside.

They told the commander that they had been shot at from the windows during their patrol. Nobody asked any questions and the incident was forgotten.

But there are scars that never heal, thought Russell as they trudged through the sand.

After what felt like an eternity, they reached a giant crater. Sergeant Niven allowed them to take a break and Russell sat down beside the woman and an older man with a moustache. Then he rummaged around in his backpack for a bottle of water before looking down into the cone-shaped abyss, hundreds of yards in diameter.

"Pretty deep hole. Could be from a meteorite, what do you think?" he turned to the woman.

"I think it's just a bomb crater," she replied.

"That's the Sedan crater," said the man with the moustache.

"What?"

"The project was called Sedan. In the 1950s an H-bomb was detonated underground. They wanted to find out if nuclear explosions could be used to create harbor basins or level out mountainous terrain for highways."

"How do you know that?" asked the woman.

"Because I worked nearby and flew over this terrain every day."

"Nearby? You mean in Area 51?" she kept probing.

"Yes, we carried out test flights with the SR-71."

"SR-71? You mean that supersonic fighter?"

"No, a supersonic reconnaissance aircraft, developed to replace the U-2. Long ago I flew the plane on missions and later in Area 51, where NASA used it as a test platform for air-breathing rocket engines."

"Hmm, doesn't look like you've gone up in the world since then," the woman said sarcastically.

"Still better than the shithole where I was three days ago."

"I have to admit, the same goes for me. I'm Ellen Slayton by the way."

"Albert Bridgeman."

Russell introduced himself, too.

"Do either of you know what all of this crap is about?" he asked after a moment's silence.

"No. The general only said that it's going to get pretty nasty. But anything's better than the gas chamber that was waiting for me in Arkansas," replied Ellen.

"Would have been a lethal injection for me. I was just waiting for the date," confessed Bridgeman.

Russell hesitated for a moment.

"I only had a few days left," he admitted. "I was completely resigned to my fate. Even now I don't hold out much hope. The general said there's not much chance of surviving this mission."

"So why didn't you just get it over and done with in jail, instead of putting yourself through this ordeal?" asked Ellen.

"A small chance is better than none. Anyway, I'd rather snuff it doing something worthwhile than just atone for the fact that I have one man's life on my conscience," retorted Russell bitterly.

"Honest answer. Most of the people in my prison claimed they were innocent."

"And what about you? Are you innocent?"

Ellen laughed defiantly. "About as innocent as

you. I would do what I did again. I had no other choice, but the jury saw it differently. You won't get any more out of me, because it's my affair and none of your damn business." Her eyes glittered with anger.

"Fair enough," Russell appeased her and turned to Albert. "And what's your excuse? Did you drop your bombs on the wrong country?"

He wasn't trying to find out what had led his comrades to death row, because it wasn't something that any prisoner liked to talk about. He just wanted to find out how thin-skinned his comrades were and who he could rely on in an emergency.

Albert stayed remarkably calm and talked openly about his past.

"Excuse?" he grunted. "I don't have an excuse. I came back from a mission two days early. I wanted to surprise my wife and entered the house quietly. She was in the shower. I could hear the noise of the water even out in the hallway. I crept into the bathroom and saw that she wasn't alone. At that moment I lost it. I stormed into the bedroom, got my gun from the closet and shot her lover in the head from behind. His brain sprayed all over her body. It was only then that I realized what I'd done."

Bridgeman didn't bat an eyelid as he told his story.

Russell shook his head. "An irrational act in the heat of the moment," he murmured to himself. "That didn't even deserve a life sentence."

"It did after the introduction of the Bigby Doctrine," retorted Bridgman with a snort. "Nowadays everyone is sentenced to death in summary trials."

Russell looked down the slope of the Sedan

crater. Albert was right. With the help of the Senate, President Bigby had quickly pushed through his campaign promise to do something about the massive rise in crime and the exploding costs of prisons. Since then, every murder and every manslaughter in the United States—whatever the motive—was given the death penalty. The same applied to rape and drug trafficking. Legal proceedings were rushed through, and appeals only granted in exceptional cases. In the past, prisoners had often waited for years on death row, whereas now it was only a matter of months between sentencing and execution. The new legislation had at first been greeted with outrage, but when the crime rate sank in record time, the protesters fell silent, and President Bigby could be sure of being reelected the following year.

All the more astounding, then, that he had now agreed to the amnesty that had led him, Russell, to the edge of this atomic bomb crater.

"Don't we need to be afraid of radiation?" he asked.

"Don't worry. The wind and weather carried off the radioactive residue long ago. But God knows how many people have died of cancer in Las Vegas because of this hole," replied Albert.

"Stand up, you bums! You've rested for long enough," yelled Corporal Barnes. "Anyone not on their feet at the count of ten will get a bullet in the head from me!"

Russell struggled back onto his aching, wobbly legs, and noticed that Albert was having even more trouble getting up.

They marched the whole afternoon and only got back to the barracks long after sundown. In front of the building, Niven got the group to stand to attention. Some of the men swayed as if they would fall down at any moment.

"Right, you scumbags. The first day is over and I'm going to tell you how things work around here. You can move freely around the compound. You've already made acquaintance with your cozy hotel rooms. That building over there is the mess." He pointed at a long, rectangular structure some distance away. "You can spend your evenings there if you're not too tired. Meals are taken there, too."

"And where's the whorehouse, Sir?" piped up a man whose forehead was traversed by a jagged scar.

"Lock Soldier Bridges in his cell," ordered Niven coolly. "No dinner today. And hand and ankle cuffs!"

The two assistant instructors led the cursing man away.

"If there's one thing I cannot abide, it's stupid jokes. Take note, you haven't seen the half of what I'm capable of. Tomorrow we start at 0500 hours with a cozy little walk to the next summit. With full backpacks, needless to say. Dismissed!"

Russell staggered to the mess, where there was a giant pot of steaming stew. He filled his bowl and sat down at a table with Ellen and Albert.

Albert looked exhausted, but Ellen still seemed relatively fit.

"You seem to be used to days like this," said Russell.

"I used to run a lot of races," she said. "I was always training and wasn't in jail long enough to get completely out of shape."

Russell looked down at his bowl and inhaled the steam. It didn't smell too bad, but after his first spoonful he grimaced. Way too salty.

A man appeared behind Ellen and started twirling strands of her hair. "Well, what have we got here? A little blond sugarplum. You should come see me tonight. Then I'll show you how ..."

"I'll give you two seconds to remove your fingers from my head, otherwise I'll break them," said Ellen in a saccharine voice.

"Head massages are my specialty. You could give me a massage, too. Ideally my ..."

In a flash, Ellen reeled around and grabbed the man's hand. There was a crunching sound as she made a jerking movement. The soldier's grin turned into a pained cry. The tray that he had been holding in his other hand sailed in a high arch across the room. Two of his fingers were bent unnaturally far back. He gritted his teeth and staggered out of the mess.

Russell grinned. "Where did you learn that?"

"I've lived my whole life in a man's world and know exactly how to deal with idiots. I'd just like to know if there are more of his kind here."

Another man sat down on the empty chair next to Russell and looked across at Ellen.

"There are a few more," he answered her question, "but Sean O'Brien is the worst."

"And who are you?" asked Russell.

"My name is James Rogers. Call me Jim."

"Right, Jim. You seem to be in the know. Enlighten us."

"I flew over here with that General Morrow. He fell asleep on the seat next to mine, so I took the opportunity to look through the dossier on the table in front of him."

"And what was in it?"

"The personal profiles of all of us 'volunteers.'"

"And?" asked Ellen.

"O'Brien, whose finger you just broke, and Michael Bridges, who's now sitting in his cell because of that stupid joke, are buddies. They held up a gas station together and shot the sales clerk. According to their psychological profiles, both are well and truly insane."

"What do you know about the others?" Russell pressed him.

"Over at that table," he said, pointing, "are Robert Walker, Vance Hilmers, and John Rushworth. Walker was a soldier and stabbed his superior after an argument. Hilmers was caught by the owner of a house during a B and E, so he shot him. Rushworth and a group of his friends blew up a Brinks truck. Unfortunately, a guard was still sitting inside. The judge didn't care that Rushworth had only been driving the getaway car." He hesitated. "And of course I also know about you lot."

Ellen winced. "Great, and who have you got on your conscience?"

"One million brave Americans."

Russell raised his eyebrows. Even he hadn't reckoned with so many. How could a single human being murder so many people? Had he ignited an atomic bomb?

"That's what the judge said, at least," Jim added. "I uploaded military secrets onto the Internet. I though America and the world should know what RedEye satellites—which the CIA and NSA are planning to shoot into space next year—are capable of."

"Never heard of them. What are they capable of?" Albert asked.

"They're infrared lasers with a sophisticated aiming system and high-resolution optics. In orbit you can use the satellites to target any person in view. You can't see the infrared laser beam and everyone will presume that the poor soul died of a stroke."

"You're kidding! Something like that is possible?"

"It's the perfect assassination tool. The secret services have spent a perverse amount of cash developing the thing. I worked for a satellite subcontractor; a colleague and I downloaded the blueprints from the server. Then I wanted to publish them on the Internet. But unfortunately the NetLeaks website was a government honeypot. I was unlucky. Even the trial took place in secret."

"Was your buddy also caught?" asked Russell.

"George Williams. Yes, he was. He's here too. He puked his guts out so much he wasn't hungry anymore. He went back to his bunk. Unfortunately, since all that happened we're not on such good terms anymore."

"Did you find anything in Morrow's papers about what this is all about?"

"Nothing revealing. But the purpose of the mission was roughly outlined in a memo. Apparently they've hidden some object here on the compound that we're supposed to test. A man died using it."

"What kind of object?" asked Ellen.

"I don't know. The memo was very vague. It only talked about the *object* and the prisoners who will carry out the *transport*."

"Transport? Then it must be some kind of

vehicle," concluded Russell.

"Or an aircraft or a missile," added Albert. "I'm a test pilot and I've also flown rocket-propelled aircraft."

"So has our astronaut here," said Jim.

Russell looked up in surprise. *Astronaut?*

He had thought Ellen was a soldier. He never would have guessed she was an astronaut. She didn't look like any astronaut he'd ever imagined.

Ellen brushed it aside. "I was a mission specialist, but I didn't fly the shuttle. I just sat at the back and was flown around in orbit. I carried out research on the International Space Station and I was a specialist for space walks and construction work. I completed my compulsory training in the T-38, but I wouldn't be suitable as a pilot."

"I have no flying experience," admitted Russell. "A few years ago I did zero-gravity combat training, but that's all. —Jim, you know the personality profiles. What's our lowest common denominator?"

"I've spent a lot of time thinking about that. We all have military training and deployment experience. Around half of us know how to fly. The rest have combat experience in exotic countries. I myself was part of Desert Storm."

"Very enlightening," said Albert sarcastically. "So they want us to fly with a mysterious object to combat missions in exotic countries. The assholes could at least tell us what they want from us."

"I don't know if it would make us feel any better," countered Russell.

Tired but overstrung, Russell sat on his bed and pondered. After a while he returned to the mess. He found some beers in the bottom drawer of the icebox and took one out. He snapped open the can, then stepped outside into the fresh air. It was dark, and he saw the guard sitting in a little hut. But he didn't look very alert, he was leafing through a magazine with a naked, busty woman on the cover.

Then from the corner of his eye, Russell noticed a movement. It came from the other side of the building. Somebody was crouching behind the trash cans watching the guard. Russell coughed deliberately loudly.

The shadow moved and stepped into the light of the setting moon. It was Sean O'Brien. His hand was bandaged.

"Are you spying on me, you motherfucker?" he asked.

Russell did not rise to the bait.

"No," he said. "I just got myself a beer and saw your shadow behind the building. What are you doing out here?"

"I would say that's none of your goddam business, jackass. Fuck off back to bed!"

"Take it easy. Why so hostile? I've got no bones to pick with you."

"Just as well, asshole. I've wiped the floor with lesser scum than you."

Russell didn't take the threat too seriously. O'Brien was about eight inches shorter than him and he didn't look very agile, either. But he didn't want to take him on if he could help it. At the same time, he asked himself why he was being so antagonistic.

"It's okay, buddy. Cool it. No sense laying into each other, we're probably going to have to get along for a while. You're Sean O'Brien, right?"

"You sure were paying attention," snarled O'Brien sarcastically.

"I'm Russell."

"Good for you." O'Brien kept glancing around with a hunted expression.

"What are you doing out here?" asked Russell calmly.

"Checking the lay of the land. Finding out how to get out of here."

"You want to escape?"

"First chance I get," O'Brien grinned.

Russell raised his eyebrows. "You know, we're all going to suffer if you screw things up."

O'Brien shrugged. "I don't give a shit. You can come with me if you want."

"I'm going to wait and see what all this is about before doing anything stupid."

"Oh I'm gonna wait a few more days, too—until things settle down here. Plus I still need to thank that blond bitch." He held up his bandaged hand.

"No need to go calling her names. You hit on her and she defended herself. Let it rest."

"I'll tell you one thing: she's going to suck my dick for what she did!"

"And I'll tell you something: Leave her alone."

"And if I don't? You going to play the hero? Wouldn't do you any good, jerk!"

Russell could feel anger welling up inside him. He had learned not to rise to the bait when he was insulted, but O'Brien was starting to go too far. He wondered if he should let it turn into a face-off. Maybe O'Brien was just a bigmouth, who would back off before things got out of hand.

But O'Brien was already backing off. "Just drink

your beer and don't get mixed up in shit that doesn't concern you, motherfucker."

His surly comrade disappeared into the barrack. Russell finished his beer and threw the can high over the fence. He'd actually drunk it in the hope that it would make him more tired, but after his conversation with O'Brien he was wide awake again.

The days that followed were awful. They marched with heavy backpacks through the desert and the nearby mountain range. They exercised until every muscle ached. The days were long and every night Russell fell into bed exhausted.

But every day he also got to know his comrades a little better. Michael Bridges and Sean O'Brien belonged to that species of asshole that makes absolutely no effort to integrate themselves into a group. They both enjoyed insulting and making fun of the others. He wasn't surprised by the fact that O'Brien, in particular, liked to torture little animals. On top of that, every few minutes he gave Ellen lustful or venomous looks. No doubt O'Brien wouldn't miss an opportunity to assault her.

Russell, on the other hand, quickly became friends with the former astronaut. They shared a pragmatic attitude and a sense of humor. He would have liked to know why Ellen had ended up on death row, but he refrained from asking any questions.

He also got on well with Jim Rogers and Albert Bridgeman. Jim was a moralist and could spend hours discussing right and wrong. The guy was obviously suffering in his present situation. Together with Ellen, Russell pepped him up whenever he was particularly down.

A few days into their stay, they were running along the edge of the Sedan crater again and Russell fell back a little with Albert.

"Was this Sedan bomb ever put to use for a civilian purpose?" Russell asked, panting.

"No, the radioactive fallout was too great. The bomb dispersed vast quantities of radioactive dust into the atmosphere—spread across half of Nevada. Las Vegas bore the brunt of it."

"Really? Never heard about that."

"Times were different then. My father spent many vacations with relatives in Nevada, and he told me that they often drove out to the mountains to watch the army carrying out nuclear tests. Once they were joined by a journalist from New York, who asked my father's uncle whether he was concerned about the children and the nuclear radiation."

"And what did the uncle say?"

"That a bit of radioactivity was good for the children and would toughen them up!"

Russell laughed. "Yes, it really was another world back then. It's a hell of a long time ago."

He liked Albert. He had a calm manner, reflected in the way he never made an unnecessary or sudden movement. In another life he would have made a convincing priest. But when he shared this thought with his companion, Albert quickly dismissed it.

"Appearances can be deceptive. I've got a lot of shit bottled up inside me; others just don't notice it. I was never one to show my feelings, even when I was young, and the rigorous training to become a pilot did the rest. Sometimes I ask myself if I have any feelings left at all. But that pile of shit inside is still seething away beneath the surface, and it can explode from one moment to the next—otherwise I wouldn't have killed my ex-wife's lover."

"It's a real weight on you, isn't it?"

"Not as much as it should be. I don't feel any sympathy for the guy. I don't know how many bombs I dropped in my ten-year military career, but I'm sure I'm responsible for hundreds of deaths. But he was the only one I had a real reason to be angry with." Albert shrugged. "I regret it because it ended up ruining my own life. Ultimately, I deserve to be executed—or to die doing whatever shit awaits us here."

"What do you think this is all about?"

"If we were all pilots here, I would say it's about kamikaze missions. But I wouldn't even trust some of the idiots in this group with a flight simulator."

Russell fell asleep quickly every night and usually woke up long before the alarm call. He often found himself stewing over things that had gone wrong in his life, about this strange mission here, and about Ellen.

He would have liked to find out more about her, but she didn't reveal much about her past. There was a vibe between them that could easily tip over into more than friendship, but in this strange group with probable death on the horizon, it didn't make much sense to succumb to your feelings.

Simple meditation exercises got him over his habit of brooding, which in Afghanistan had nearly sent him into a depression. He had learned to meditate from a comrade of Indian descent who had been shot dead during his final mission. During his meditation training he had learned to concentrate on the moment and to be aware of his thoughts. When unwelcome images popped into his head, he gently pushed them aside until he had achieved a state of serene emptiness. He would then remain in this state as if he were drifting on a cloud. Ravi had called this mindfulness. It had helped him not only during the war but also in prison, when in the confines of his cell the thought of his impending execution had driven him almost over the edge.

4. The Transporter

The following day there were no morning exercises. When they lined up in front of the building after breakfast, General Morrow was standing beside Sergeant Niven to greet the group. Russell knew that the drill was now over. Finally they would find out what this was all about.

"Good morning, soldiers. I'm pleased to see you looking in much better shape. You've got more color, you're clearly fitter, and I can assure you that you will need to be in good shape. I know you're asking yourselves why the President let you out of jail. Today you're going to find out what this project is all about."

"Well, it's about time," murmured Jim Rogers.

"What lies in store for you will sound pretty unbelievable if I *tell* you. So I've decided to simply *show* you. I suggest you get your belongings and climb aboard that truck over there. You're moving to new quarters and won't be coming back here."

Minutes later, they were all sitting in the back of the army truck. They drove for half an hour through the desert to the edge of the mountains, where a few buildings stood in front of the entrance to a tunnel. The buildings had obviously been erected in a hurry. One of them was still covered in scaffolding. The tunnel, on the other hand, had clearly been around for a while, its concrete walls were covered in moss. Heavily armed guards were protecting the entrance.

The general pointed at the buildings. "That's where you'll be living while you prepare for your mission. You can move around the compound freely and there are various amenities for you."

"Can we call our families?" asked George

Williams. Since the breach of secrecy they had carried out together, Jim Rogers's former partner had kept his distance. Russell had barely talked to him.

"No. That won't be possible," replied General Morrow. "The project is top secret. Your families have been informed that you volunteered for a military mission, and that if you survive you will be granted amnesty. You will have no contact with the outside world. Cell phones are forbidden within the compound and signals are blocked by jammers in any case. There are also no cable connections for the Internet or phones. We are sealed off from the outside world except for a data connection to the Pentagon, and only I have access authorization."

"So what's this all about?"

"You will find out shortly. Please be patient for a few minutes."

They passed the guards in front of the dark entrance to the tunnel. Soldiers raised the barriers for the truck and carried a barrier to the side. The guards stared at the group wide-eyed. Almost in awe.

They know what this is about. Goddammit, what's waiting for us in this tunnel?

"This facility is a leftover from the Cold War," said Morrow, as they drove down a narrow road in the tunnel "It's taking us to an underground chamber about a mile below ground."

After about five minutes the truck came to a halt. The end of the tunnel was sealed with a solid steel bulkhead, which opened at his command. They drove for several more feet and then stopped, as the heavy door closed behind them.

Russell climbed out and looked around the big cave in awe. It was at least a mile and a half in diameter, and had a half-moon shape.

"This cavern was melted into the rocks by an H-bomb at the beginning of the Sixties. You're already familiar with the Sedan crater from your training. An explosive charge of a similar strength was used here. However, it took five years for the radioactivity to reach a low enough level for us to put the cave to any use. That was longer than we'd expected. There is still some residual radiation but it won't harm you."

Russell looked around him. Everywhere there were tents, office containers, generators and vehicles. Cables crisscrossed the bare concrete ground.

There were only a few people in the cave besides them. A few soldiers stood around the entrance, and engineers were talking with technicians in white lab coats next to a device mounted on a tripod. Floodlights lit up the entire cave. Most of them were directed at the middle of the cave. And then Russell saw the strange object.

"What the hell is that?" said Vance Hilmers in awe.

Now everyone was looking wide-eyed toward the center of the cave. The object was at first no more than a black surface in Russell's field of vision. It was so dark and shapeless it felt as if he had a floater in his eye. It was only as he moved closer that he could make out shades of gray. The thing was spherical in shape and had a diameter of about thirty feet. There was some scaffolding set up on one side of the object.

The general stood in front of the thing and indicated to the group not to move closer.

"A few months ago we found this object at the bottom of the ocean off the coast of California. A gravimetric expedition that was underway discovered a mass concentration at a depth of six thousand feet. Eventually a salvage vessel hauled the object up to the surface and initial investigations revealed a cavity within the sphere. You can open it by laying your hand on the outer surface."

Morrow demonstrated, and an opening of about fifteen-by-fifteen feet appeared as if from nowhere beside the spot where the general had placed his hand.

"Follow me."

Dumbfounded, Russell stepped into the mysterious object. Its outer shell was barely a quarter of an inch thick, like the skin of a blister. Inside, the wall had a grayish color and emitted a strange and surreal light. Floating in the middle of the domed space was a smaller sphere with a diameter of about twelve feet. Aircraft steps had been set up to reach the second sphere.

"The little sphere up there is also hollow. You can enter it in the same way, by laying your hand on the wall. An opening appears almost immediately. But don't ask me how it is able to float up there: unfortunately we have no idea as yet."

"What is it? Who built it?" asked Vance Hilmers.

"We assume that it is an alien object."

There was suppressed laughter in the background.

"And what makes you think that?"

"Dr. Gilbert will explain that to you. He is our head physicist and scientific project manager." Morrow nodded at a gaunt man who had entered the sphere after them. He was wearing a white lab coat. Beneath it you could see a gray shirt and an ugly, sloppily done-up tie. In his hand he was holding a notebook and the lenses of his glasses were solid blocks.

"Good afternoon gentlemen. Ah, and lady. Now that you have had a good look at our treasure, I will tell you everything we know—right, General?"

"Go ahead, Gilbert. There's no need for secrecy here."

"Good," said the project manager and turned to face the group. "The object has an outside diameter of thirty-eight feet and an inside diameter of forty-one feet." He paused dramatically, before continuing. "Yes, you heard correctly, the inside diameter is bigger than the outside diameter."

"Completely impossible," said Ellen. "How could that be?"

"We assume that the outer shell causes a curvature of space, similar to what one would expect to find in the proximity of a black hole. And that is not the only peculiarity."

Russell listened in disbelief.

Black holes? What the hell is he talking about? What on earth have they got their hands on?

He glanced down uncertainly at the shell of the sphere on which he was standing. If he shifted his weight, he could feel the surface giving way slightly. He closed his eyes and tried to digest what he was hearing.

"We found the object while making gravimetric analyses of the ocean floor. Based on a measurement of its gravitational field, it has a mass of around five by ten to the power of twelve kilograms, which is a little more than the mass of Mount Everest. You could compare it to a small planetoid. But in fact it only weighs about twenty thousand tons, otherwise, of course, we could not have salvaged it from the ocean bed."

"And what is the thing made of?" Jim Rogers now ventured to ask.

"We don't know."

"Didn't you carry out a spectroscopic analysis?"

"We tried everything: X-rays, gamma, laser, neutrons, alpha rays. The lot. This material absorbs absolutely everything. We tried to scratch the outer skin with a diamond, even that didn't work."

"What about electromagnetic radiation?"

"Doesn't penetrate the skin. It's all absorbed. Although the object itself produces radiation in the gigahertz range. We assume that this rapidly changing magnetic field is what causes the headaches that you are probably all experiencing. Strangely, it is only present inside the sphere. But the radiation level is low, so it is unlikely to cause any biological damage."

Russell and Ellen exchanged glances. Only now did he notice that he really did have a slight headache.

What kind of a weird thing is this?

"And? Have you worked out what it's for?" asked Rushworth.

Russell looked expectantly at the physicist, who nodded slowly.

"Yes, it appears to be a transportation device."

"You mean, this thing can move? Is it a spaceship?"

"No, the object itself doesn't move. But it is capable of transporting humans who are inside the small, floating sphere. The sphere is clearly a teleportation device."

"Incredible!" whispered Russell.

"Are you fucking with us?" asked Vance Hilmers.

"And where does it take you?" Ellen probed.

Gilbert went up to a black column that stuck a several feet out of the ground like a branch from a tree trunk. The surface was completely smooth and black, and a series of strange symbols glowed on it.

"You can select your destination with this. Then the person to be transported enters the inner sphere, closes it and presses a button on a similar column, which sets the teleportation in motion. You can also control the process from this column. Two of my colleagues found this out by chance when they carried out a series of tests with the device."

"And where can you go with it?"

The general, who had stayed in the background for the last few minutes, stepped forward and looked at the group.

"It takes you to similar spheres in other solar systems; that much we have been able to determine so far. It will be your job to find out where exactly— by letting yourself be teleported with this contraption."

Russell could feel his head spinning. So that was the big secret. He'd spent a lot of time over the last few weeks wondering what this mission could be about. He'd come up with some pretty far-fetched theories, but he never would have imagined something of this enormity.

Unbelievable.

General Morrow left the group alone and announced that there would be a meeting in the afternoon with further details.

Afterwards, Dr. Gilbert showed them around the cave a little more and explained some of the measuring devices that were set up around the mysterious sphere. Finally, the truck brought the group back up to the surface and to their new quarters.

Russell threw his duffel bag on the bed, still stunned by what he had seen in the cave. Surprisingly few questions had been asked. Obviously the prisoners needed to digest the news first.

He looked out of the window and could see the entrance to the tunnel. A truck loaded with equipment was passing by the security barrier.

The new living quarters were much more comfortable than the barracks where they had spent the last few weeks. Each volunteer had a private room with a bed, desk, locker, and a small washroom. What's more, the doors to the rooms could be locked.

The common area also suggested that they had all moved up a level. Down the corridor was a kitchen and a larger rec room with a TV and a fridge filled with drinks.

Russell lay down on his bed still wearing his uniform, his heavy, booted feet dangled over the edge of the mattress. Pensively he closed his eyes and immediately saw the spooky black sphere. In a few days, he would climb into that strange thing and be teleported—to the stars.

5. The Ugly Truth

A few men had gathered in the kitchen, talking agitatedly. Shortly afterwards, General Morrow entered the room with Dr. Gilbert and told the group to follow them.

They fetched the others from their rooms and walked over to the neighboring building, which was a little larger and had two stories. Here they sat down in a conference room where the tables had been arranged in a horseshoe formation. A projector cast the Air Force logo on the wall. While General Morrow prepared to start talking, the physicist busied himself with a laptop.

"You've seen the object and now you know what you're doing here. You've had a few hours to digest the news and will now doubtlessly have many questions. The time has come to go into more detail."

An image appeared on the wall. It showed a tugboat being pulled into a harbor by a warship. A spherical object was lying on the boat covered in canvas.

"Some years ago, the big outer tanks of the space shuttles were towed from the factory near New Orleans to Cape Canaveral. We borrowed the ship from NASA to get the object to Vandenberg in California. From there it was brought here by superload truck."

"Why to the cave specifically?" asked Albert.

"Because it was the best place to hide it. And the surrounding rock, which is several miles thick, blocks the sphere's electromagnetic radiation, which our Chinese friends might otherwise have detected with their satellites."

"And how did you work out that it's a teleportation device?"

"We will come to that shortly."

An image of the cave was projected on the wall. The strange object was clear to see. Two technicians in lab coats stood in front of the sphere, placed their hands on it, created an opening and disappeared inside. Now the image changed to one of the inside of the sphere.

"All activity in the cave and in the object itself is recorded constantly by a dozen surveillance cameras. The men who you can see in the picture are two of our engineers. On the left, at the control column, is Mr. Blumberg. You'll meet him later on. He is responsible for the technical facilities in the cave and is in charge of the measuring devices. The man now going up the steps and disappearing into the little sphere is Gordon Evans. Unfortunately you will no longer get to know him."

Russell could feel his shoulders tensing. He could guess why he would no longer meet this Evans, and the general's next words confirmed his suspicion.

"At the time when this was filmed we presumed that the object was a kind of communications device," explained Gilbert. "Since no electromagnetic radiation can penetrate the inside of the smaller sphere, and thereby no radio contact is possible, we assumed that one could establish a communications link with the columns. Mr. Evans had an idea that he wanted to try out inside the little sphere. Now pay attention: Here you can see how one of the symbols on the control pillar changes when Mr. Blumberg touches it with his finger. And now he's pressing on the illuminated panel below it. This is obviously what triggered the teleportation. As you can see, next to the illuminated panel he just pressed, another one appears to its left."

Russell craned his neck to get a better look. On the screen he could see Blumberg picking up a camera and photographing the column from different angles. The engineer paused for a moment, as though wondering what to do next, before pressing again on the first panel. Then he called something out to the technician, who quickly ran up the steps and created an opening in the little sphere. The perspective of the camera did not precisely reveal what was going on inside, but there was frantic activity. Men in uniform and lab coats ran up the steps and leant over something inside the sphere. Finally they carried a lifeless bundle down the steps.

The engineer Evans, thought Russell.

"What happened to the man?" he asked.

Physicist Gilbert opened another file. "I will now show you the recording of the surveillance camera from inside the transporter sphere."

A new film began. Russell could see the engineer entering the little sphere and closing the opening. For a few minutes he was occupied with a measuring device until his eyes suddenly opened wide and he clutched his chest. His legs no longer touched the ground but floundered helplessly in the air. With his right foot he kicked the device next to him, which then slowly floated upward.

Russell had never seen anybody gaping with such wide eyes—it looked as if his eyeballs would pop out of their sockets at any moment. The man appeared to scream, but nothing could be heard over the loudspeakers. He started to turn blue while still clutching his chest. Thick drops of blood oozed out of his nose, which first collected as beads on the end of his nose and then floated off in every direction. The engineer turned bluer in the face. His tongue swelled grotesquely out of his mouth, while his body turned slowly on its axis. It looked as if he was lying in an invisible hammock and floundering with his hands and feet. Then suddenly, like a wet sack, the engineer fell to the ground where he remained motionless. After a few minutes the sphere opened and men came inside to examine the lifeless body, shaking their heads in confusion and finally carrying the technician away.

Russell turned round to George Williams. His comrade had turned pale and looked as if he was about to throw up. "What was that? What happened to him?"

"The physiological symptoms and the subsequent examination suggest that the man was subjected to a vacuum for around one-and-a-half minutes."

Russell turned around in his chair. Standing by the door was an older man with straggly, shoulder-length gray hair. He had a narrow face and was wearing a shabby gray suit.

"May I present Dr. Darren Cummings? He has been assigned as the doctor for our project and will be taking care of you over the coming weeks," said Morrow.

"Thank you, General," the doctor replied. He walked around the table and stood next to Morrow. "I carried out the examination of the body following this incident and was quickly able to determine the cause of death. The man's body temperature continued to drop very fast, which suggested an ambient temperature of over minus three-hundred degrees Fahrenheit. That he was subjected to zero gravity you could see for yourselves."

"You would have been better off sending an astronaut into the sphere!" commented Russell.

"That's exactly what we did." The general smiled.

Meanwhile Gilbert opened a new file. Once again the inside of the sphere could be seen. A man in a space suit stepped through the opening. He was carrying a big box, which he put down next to the control column before closing the opening again from inside.

"We asked NASA for help, and they sent us some of their former astronauts from the Shuttle Program," said Gilbert. "This man here is Colonel Holbrook. At the time we still didn't think we were dealing with a transporter. In fact, we believed that the control column could be set to create different atmospheric conditions inside the sphere. Like in an atmosphere chamber. But see for yourselves."

The astronaut began fiddling around with the pillar and became suddenly weightless—like the engineer before him. The space suit protected him against the vacuum. Now he turned his attention to the box he had taken in with him and began flipping various switches.

"We set the control pillar the same way as before. The idea was for Colonel Holbrook to make precise measurements of the conditions inside the sphere. He also wanted to try and open the wall of the inner sphere."

Russell watched with interest. An opening appeared in the wall and the astronaut looked out for a long time. Then he took a camera that was attached to his suit and took several photos. The film didn't show what was outside the opening.

Now there was a change of scene: what could be seen appeared to be the outer cavity, but the equipment and the people were gone.

"Only now did it dawn on the astronaut that he was somewhere else. He felt his way to the edge of the outer sphere and created an opening here, too. It was from this perspective that he took the following pictures."

The image now projected on the wall could have come from the Apollo moon landing: a gray, slightly rippled surface with small craters covered in a fine dust. The horizon seemed very close. Stars twinkled up above.

Russell gathered his thoughts. It was incredible. You stepped into this strange sphere, tapped something on the control panel and suddenly found yourself on a far-away planet. He found it almost impossible to believe. It was too much like science fiction.

"Fortunately, Colonel Holbrook was able to return with the help of the control device."

The physicist projected an image of the black control pillar onto the wall. On the pillar was a disk with a series of symbols.

"It's a like a number combination. By pressing on the symbols, you can scroll through different options. Basically it's like a touchscreen. Every symbol combination represents a particular destination. The combination that you can see here is for our sphere here on Earth. Following a transport, the symbols always jump back to this value. You should take good note of it."

"Are you trying to say that the damn thing works like a phone booth? You go in, dial a number and—*puff!*—you're on the moon?"

"You hit the nail on the head, Mr. Bridges." General Morrow's sarcastic tone made it clear what he thought of Bridge's impertinent attitude.

A new image appeared on the wall: a black sphere, identical to the one down in the cave, was resting in the middle of the lunar landscape. It looked like a futuristic landing capsule.

"Colonel Holbrook took this photo during another expedition. He also took a series of photos of the sky so that we can work out the position of this planet in relation to the stars."

"Is he on the moon? Where's Earth?"

"This sphere is not on the moon—that much we know for sure. There is less gravity on our moon than there is on Earth, but you aren't completely weightless. We thought that it was perhaps an asteroid or a small moon in the outer solar system."

"Yeah, and?"

"The night sky is very different from the one we see from Earth. This photo was taken neither in our nor in a neighboring solar system."

There was a murmur of voices as some of the men began talking among themselves. Ellen leaned over to Russell. "That's the craziest thing I've ever heard. Every astronaut would jump at the chance to explore the worlds that this thing could take them to."

Russell nodded his head thoughtfully. He had come to the same conclusion. He pushed himself back from the table and stood up. Everyone in the room turned to look at him.

"With all due respect, Sir. You said you got astronauts from NASA to explore these worlds. So why do you need us?"

Everyone turned to look at the general. Morrow didn't speak; then he turned to Dr. Gilbert and nodded. The physicist nodded back before opening another video file.

An astronaut in a space suit could be seen sitting on a chair and pulling his helmet on. He struggled with the latch for a few seconds until a technician in blue overalls came to his assistance. In the background—slightly blurred—you could see the sphere.

"That is Captain Summers, a former test pilot and shuttle pilot. After Colonel Holbrook had been on several transports to the planetoid, Summers suggested selecting a different symbol configuration, which would take him to a different destination." Dr. Gilbert adjusted his spectacles. His voice was brittle, as if he was fighting his memories. "Captain Peter Summers was a happy go lucky kind of guy. He was always in a good mood and his optimism was infectious. He was a young man full of energy and the first person to come forward for a new adventure."

The physicist paused. Meanwhile the astronaut in the film had put on his helmet. He flipped up the visor and looked at the cameraman.

"Hey, Ridley. Make sure you film this!" he called. "I'm gonna show it to my wife when I get back and the mission is declassified. She thinks I'm playing poker on some aircraft carrier."

Somebody laughed in the background. Now the astronaut looked straight into the camera. With his short blond hair, his intelligent and alert blue eyes, and his winning smile he could have talked anybody into anything, thought Russell.

"Hey Sweetie, I'm on my way to the stars! In a few minutes I'll be further away than you can imagine. You see this here?" Summers held up a neck-chain with a locket: "I'm going to fill this with stardust and lay it at your feet!" Now the daredevil astronaut looked into the camera a little more seriously. "I love you!"

A technician behind him was grinning in amusement. The astronaut turned around and marched to the sphere with two technicians.

Dr. Gilbert cleared his throat. "We treated the number combination like a phone number and simply changed the last digit by one number. We thought the first symbols might be some kind of area code. That's why we thought that by changing the last number we would be selecting a destination close to the first one. We were hoping we could work out a system, or reach a destination where we could find out more information about the sphere and its function."

Now Captain Summers had reached the outer sphere and disappeared inside with the two technicians. The scene changed to the outer cavity. In the foreground, on the left, the engineers were standing at the control column; in the background, on the right, Summers was standing at the top of the steps. In front of the opening to the inner sphere he struck a pose, glanced back briefly, and pulled down the visor of his helmet. A broad smile was the last one saw of his face. Then he stretched out his hand and stuck up his thumb. One of the technicians returned the gesture as the devil-may-care astronaut disappeared into the sphere and closed the opening by touching the wall beside it.

"We had arranged with Captain Summers that once he had been transported, he would analyze the environmental atmosphere and return within five minutes," explained Gilbert. "Once the teleportation has been initiated, the connection remains until it is broken off either by us or by the person in the transporter. This is done by pressing on a panel on the control pillar. Only then can the inner porthole be opened."

"And what happened to Summers?" asked Jim.

"We were still connected, but the Captain didn't return. So we transported him back from our end, which is possible at any time as long as there is still a connection."

The technician in the film sequence pressed on an area of the control pillar and waited. For several minutes they stared at the sphere, but Summers did not emerge. Agitatedly they discussed what they should do. Finally one of them went up the steps. He stopped in front of the outer wall of the inner sphere and tentatively touched it. An opening appeared through which he looked into the capsule. The film didn't show what he saw but for some time the technician peered inside with a puzzled expression. Suddenly his eyes widened. With a jerk he turned around and vomited on the steps in front of his feet.

"First time you've seen a pussy?" joked Bridges uncertainly.

The scene changed again and showed a photo of the inside of the little sphere.

"But it's empty!" gasped John Rushworth. "What happened to the Captain?"

"And where does that red color come from?" asked Ellen, because the floor of the sphere was red, as if it had been neatly painted.

"That red color," Cummings began in a hoarse voice, "was all that remained of Captain Summers."

You could have heard a pin drop. Sean O'Brien stared at the doctor open-mouthed, while a look of horror spread across Ellen's face. Russell's mind was whirring frantically. What the hell could be responsible for that mess?

After what felt like an eternity, Dr. Cummings went round to the laptop and searched for a file in one of the folders. He found it and enlarged it on the wall. It was a grayscale image. Russell couldn't see exactly what it was of. It looked like a pile of logs that somebody had hastily thrown together.

"This is an electron-microscopic image," explained Cummings. "The slivers that you can see here are tiny fragments of bone. Summers' bones. We were able to extract them from the red color. They have a diameter of less than a micrometer."

"Have you found out how it could have happened?" asked Jim Rogers.

"We carried out finite element analyses and worked out the force required to break up bones into fragments of that size." The doctor paused and scanned the men's faces. His gaze lingered on Ellen. "We assume that Captain Summers emerged in an environment in which the gravitational force was tenthousand to twelvethousand times as strong as on Earth. Perhaps he landed on a neutron star or the surface of a solidified white dwarf. I have no idea. In any case, he was dead within a fraction of a second. Soldiers had to remove the remains from the wall with sanding machines. There was nothing left except for that red crust. Even the tiniest screw from his equipment had been fragmented into tiny pieces. I wouldn't have thought it was possible that ..."

The general interrupted the doctor with a wave of the hand: "You can imagine that after this transport, none of our astronauts wanted to pick a random number." He looked Russell directly in the eyes. "I guess you can now understand why we had to fall back on convicts like you."

His words were followed by a silence that was eventually broken by Sean O'Brien.

"If you think I'm going to set one foot in your machine from hell, then you've got another thing coming!"

"In that case, Mr. O'Brien, you will be taken straight to the nearest military prison and executed in the evening, as was your fate to begin with. You are now under military command, and refusal to obey orders is subject to immediate punishment under martial law—with the express authorization of the President and on his directive."

"What do you assholes think you can get away with? Do you seriously believe that I'm going to go and sit in that death capsule and be voluntarily blasted to hell? Are you crazy?"

"Yes, Mr. O'Brien, I do think that. In jail, I told you quite honestly that the chances of survival on this mission are minimal. And you accepted."

"Accepted to be mashed to pulp?" screamed O'Brien. "This is bullshit! I thought this was a combat operation!"

Others nodded in agreement and angry murmuring broke out.

"Why don't you first test the transporter—or whatever you want to call it—on machines and examine the environments with probes or something?" suggested Russell. "Then you can still send a human if you want to."

"That doesn't work," said Dr. Gilbert. "The transport can't be started unless a person is in the chamber. We don't know why that is."

"Do you mean the thing only transports animate beings? Then how come the space suit is also transported?"

"I didn't say that. Of course the contraption transports inanimate matter, but only if a human is also on board."

"Then beam a goddamn chimpanzee!" shouted O'Brien.

"We did in fact try that. It doesn't work. We believe that the device only responds to very intelligent life. We even put in a pool with a dolphin, but that didn't work either. Sending a dead human also doesn't work. We had a corpse brought to us from a nearby funeral parlor and tried putting it in the sphere."

"Holy shit!"

"So just to get this straight," said Michael Bridges, rising to his feet. "You motherfuckers want to choose any old number on that thing, which could take us God knows where, and we're expected to get in and be turned into pulp? Are you completely nuts?"

"Calm down—and please sit back down."

Reluctantly, Bridges sat down. O'Brien remained standing for a few more moments, red in the face, before also lowering himself into his seat again.

"Why the hurry?" asked Russell. "Why don't you study the thing until you've understood the system behind it? Bring in other, better scientists. Then you'll get to the bottom of how that thing works."

The general reached for a piece of paper. "The order comes right from the top. The President wants us to solve the mystery of this contraption as quickly as possible?"

"Why?"

"We don't know if another nation also has a thing like this hidden away in some bunker. If there's one sphere on this Earth, there might be more. The designers of this thing are technologically far more advanced than we are, and he who masters it will have a vast amount of power over all humanity. And there's another reason: How can we be sure that it won't burst open one day and spew out an invading army? Whether aliens or the Chinese, there would be dramatic consequences. No, Harris. We have to get to the bottom of the secret of the transporter—as quickly as possible. We've tried out everything we could. Either we have to work out the system of the destination combination, or we need to reach a place where we can find the answers."

O'Brien was whispering loudly with Bridges. His face was still flushed, but the general was unperturbed.

"Our offer still stands. Each of you will carry out ten transports and document the environment you get to. With every mission, you face the risk of death. But you have a chance of coming back in one piece. And if that is the case, you are free. Up to now we have only selected two destinations, of which only one proved to be fatal. There is therefore a fifty percent chance of survival for every mission—that is relatively high. In the Second World War there were bombing missions in German airspace with a lower chance of survival. And don't forget that you would have died for sure in jail. All of you are welcome to reconsider. It is your decision."

The general stuffed his papers in a bag and reached for his hat, which was lying on the table in front of him. "I would say that's all for today. Tomorrow we will begin the intensive training. You will be familiarized with the pressure suits and the technology. In preparation, each of you will be transported to the planetoid discovered by Holbrook, whose combination we know and where we are currently setting up a small manned station. There you will learn to work in a vacuum and zero gravity. We will prepare you as well as we possibly can."

The general scanned everybody's faces one last time. Then he turned on his heel and marched out of the room.

6. Hiatus

No sooner had the general left the room than an animated discussion broke out. O'Brien, in particular, stirred things up.

"The motherfuckers can't do this to us! They're throwing us into their hellish machine like guinea pigs and will have a good laugh when we end up as mush on the floor. We won't do it! We'll fight back!"

"And how do you envisage doing that?" asked Ellen.

"We'll disarm the guards and get the hell out of here."

"And how do you intend to do that, you bigmouth? How do we fight the whole camp with a few men?"

"Bitch, you can die in that thing for all I care. But first you can suck my cock."

"Hey," said Russell. "Ellen is right, and you know it. I don't want to climb into that thing either, but I agree with the general that someone has to get in there and look for some answers. I'm thankful to have the opportunity. If this alien object didn't exist, I would have been dead a week ago."

He asked himself if he really believed what he was saying. The idea of getting into the sphere, pressing the panel, and not knowing if he would be turned to dust in the next second, was terrifying. But purely out of principle he didn't want to agree with O'Brien. He also hated the way that asshole hit on Ellen.

"Then you can cry *thank you* when you get into that machine from hell, Mr. super-soldier! And you can take your babe in with you."

Russell frowned. His *babe?*

"You don't need to gawp like that! A blind person can see that you're after the bitch."

Ellen blushed.

That's enough!

He stood up and walked over to O'Brien. He didn't want to start a fight, but if O'Brien carried on like that he would have to teach him a lesson.

"Oh, what do we have here? Is our elite soldier getting a little bit pissed? Can't handle the truth, eh?"

"That could be, but you obviously can't deal with reality. Morrow is expecting this. He's just waiting for one of us to do something stupid. I can guarantee you they've got the whole area staked out down to the last inch, and the old nuclear test site is hundreds of square miles in size. You won't even get close to the boundary fence. And then the general will make an example of you and shoot you. So think about it. If we get into the transporter at least we stand a chance."

"You call that a chance? It's a game of Russian roulette! Not with me. I'm getting out of here!"

"Anyway, what are the chances that we survive the missions?" asked Rushworth. "They tried out two destinations. One of them would kill us, the other not. That means a fifty-fifty chance. If it continues like that, what are the chances of surviving the ten transports that we're supposed to do? —Albert?"

Rushworth turned to look at Albert, whose face was scrunched up in concentration. Obviously he was working it out in his head.

"With two missions, the chances of surviving would be one to four. With three missions one to eight and so on. With ten missions, the chances are one to a thousand and twenty-four."

O'Brien laughed shrilly. "And you call that a chance, jerk? That isn't a chance, it's certain death! None of us will survive our ten missions, and that's exactly what they want!"

"No, I don't believe that," said Albert. "The data pool for the probability of one to two is too low. It could well be that this neutron star was an exception and that all the rest are far lower-risk. Or there's a chance one of us finds an instruction manual on our first mission or some clue as to how the thing works."

"I couldn't give a shit! I'm not getting into that thing, I'm out of here!"

"Let's see how the first transports go. Then maybe we'll know more."

"Then why don't you volunteer and do your ten missions one after the other! If you're still alive at the end, I might reconsider!"

"That brings me to another point," said Albert. "In what order are we supposed to get into that thing?"

"The one with the shortest dick can go first," sneered O'Brien. "And the little cunt there is welcome to be squished first." He stormed out, and the discussion came to an end.

Russell lay awake in his bed. He pondered over the day's events and his chances of getting out of here alive. He asked himself if it had really been a good idea to sign up for this project. It would have been easier to die in jail. Then it would all be over now. He was scared shitless by the thought of climbing into that machine and not knowing which hell he might be transported to.

Since he knew he wouldn't be able to sleep, he got up to grab some fresh air. He wasn't the only one. Outside, Jim Rogers was smoking a cigarette, lost in thought and staring up at the stars. When Jim noticed him he smiled and rummaged around in his bag. His comrade held out a packet of cigarettes towards him.

"I actually quit in Afghanistan, but fuck it. Tar in the lungs is the least of my problems right now." Russell helped himself to a smoke. Jim handed him a lighter and Russell inhaled deeply. He immediately felt dizzy.

Oh Jesus. My first cigarette in three years. I should have known better.

He spluttered and took another puff, then looked straight at his comrade. "How did you get your hands on these?"

"I wheedled them off a guard." Jim shrugged. "Some of those guys feel for us. They know exactly why we're here." He took a deep drag and blew little white plumes of smoke into the air. "I bet none of us will get a good night's sleep tonight."

"What do you think about all this shit?"

"I have no idea what I should be thinking. The whole thing is crazy. We found this thing that gives us access to the Milky Way, and nobody bothered to provide an instruction manual."

"Yup, and now we're the guinea pigs. I have a feeling that Morrow, and that Gilbert guy, know exactly how they could work out the system of the number combination. The only question is, how many of us will die first."

"There are a few things I don't get. I may not be a physicist, but I am an engineer and have got a bit of an idea about technology. But I really don't have a clue how that whatchamacallit could work. I especially don't get how it could know if there's a human being or something else inside. What's the point of that?"

"Perhaps the aliens don't want us to beam bombs to their planets."

"That's another point. Who built the thing? Why was it lying down there at the bottom of the ocean and for how long? A week? A thousand years? A hundred million years?" Jim shook his head. "It's crazy, totally crazy." He threw his cigarette butt on the ground and immediately lit another one. "So, Russell, what do you think of O'Brien? Do you reckon he could get us into trouble?"

"I get where he's coming from. He doesn't want to get into that thing, and I wouldn't put it past him to do something stupid to avoid it. We should keep an eye on him."

"And what about you? I get the impression you couldn't care less if you die in that thing or not."

Russell shrugged. He tried to come up with a good answer, but couldn't find one. Nonetheless, Jim nodded understandingly.

"When you've been through as much shit as you have, it's hardly surprising if you lose the will to live," said Jim,

Russell looked at him in surprise. He had never spoken to Jim about his past.

"You know that I read the files."

Russell nodded. "You're right. Ever since that day I've struggled just to get up in the morning. I should have stayed in jail. It would have all been behind me by now." He flicked the butt away. Jim offered him another one, but he declined.

Jim hesitated. "You know that quite a few of the people here have been through a lot. You realize that, don't you?"

Russell shrugged ambivalently. He knew Albert's story, but didn't know if he should really feel sorry for him.

"I mean Ellen," explained his comrade. "She asked about you. Don't be angry with me, but I told her your story. At least the gist of it."

Russell could feel anger welling up in him. It was his past and he would have chosen the right moment to tell Ellen. In his own words.

"I'm sorry Russell, really."

He didn't want to be angry with Jim. He didn't want to lose it like he had on that fateful day. And he had to admit, he was pleased that Ellen had asked about him.

"Would you like to know how Ellen ended up here?" asked Jim, leaning forward confidentially. "It would only be fair for me to tell you."

For a moment Russell was tempted to give in to his curiosity, but he decided against it.

"No, Jim. It's okay. I'll ask her myself. Just give me another smoke and we're quits."

Jim held out the pack again. They stood next to other in silence for some time and smoked their cigarettes.

7. The Space Suit

"That's an EMU. EMU stands for Extravehicular Mobility Unit, which is a standard space suit for extravehicular activity on the International Space Station—alongside the Russian ORLON suit of course. The complete model with backpack weighs around two-hundred-and-eighty pounds and can keep an astronaut alive for at least eight hours in a vacuum."

Colonel Christian Holbrook was showing the group a white space suit mounted on a metal stand. They stood around him in a semicircle. In the background, General Morrow leant against a wall and watched the proceedings.

"Since we train with it in a pool, it also helps against excess pressure or if you come out in a liquid—although the pressure can't be too high, of course."

"It didn't save your friend from ending up as red paste in that shit sphere," scoffed O'Brien.

Holbrook looked up briefly, but did not respond to the remark. He moved on a few steps to another space suit.

"Because a normal space suit is too heavy to wear in Earth's gravity, we have considerably reduced the weight of this suit here. Consequently it will only keep you alive for an hour. You will wear this suit on your transport. We're using the other one for longer trips to destinations where we know there is zero gravity. Of course, so far we only know of one destination of this kind: the Summers Planetoid."

"The what planetoid?"

"We named the small planet discovered on the

first expedition after astronaut Peter Summers. We've started to set up a little station there, which, with the help of the transporter, we intend to have permanently manned."

"Why, for Chrissake?"

"So that our astronauts can practice using the transporter. And with the help of a telescope, we want a team of scientists to find out where this planetoid is situated in relation to the surrounding stars."

"That's great," said Michael Bridges sarcastically.

"I'm glad you think so, Mr. Bridges. Because it's where you'll be headed on your first transport." Holbrook turned to Ellen, who was standing next to him. "It's nice to see you again, Ellen. I'm glad they got you out of jail. You really didn't deserve a fate like that." He hesitated. "Although I'm not sure whether being here is much better."

"I would rather risk my life on a mission to space than wait to die in a tiny cell."

Holbrook nodded understandingly.

"You already know how to use a space suit, and nothing's changed since you've been gone. Perhaps you can help me to show your comrades how to use the EMU?"

"Sure Chris, I'd be glad to." They hugged briefly and Holbrook patted her on the back.

Russell felt a pang of jealousy. They obviously knew each other well. He presumed that Holbrook had worked with Ellen on the space station program before he had been transferred here.

After Holbrook's introduction they divided up into several groups. First, Colonel Rogers showed them how to use the suit. Ellen called Russell over.

"You know how to use these things?" he asked.

"Yes, very well in fact. I carried out several extravehicular missions at the International Space Station in one of these suits—not counting the hundreds of hours of training at JSC."

"JSC?"

"The Johnson Space Center in Houston. That's where we were prepared for our flights—it has a big training pool. At the bottom of the pool there's a model of the space station where we could practice our missions."

"A model of the whole space station? Then the pool must be huge."

"It puts every Olympic pool to shame!" Ellen grinned. "In the water we can simulate zero gravity. After you've trained in the pool for hundreds of hours, it doesn't seem that strange when you finally start to work outside on the modules of the space station. After a while you practically forget that you're floating two-hundred-and-fifty miles above the Earth."

"Must have been an amazing job."

"The best there is!"

Russell still didn't know what his colleague had been convicted of. He had hoped she would come round to talking about it herself, but she avoided the subject. He decided to give her a little nudge.

"Must have been a long journey from up there to here."

Ellen narrowed her eyes slightly. Then she nodded slowly. "I know what you're getting at. And it's only fair if I tell you how I ended up in jail, since Jim told me your story."

He didn't answer.

"I like you, Russell. And I think you like me too. I would like to talk to you about it at some point, but not here and not now." She considered whether she should continue, and finally said: "I'm scared. I'm scared of what lies ahead of us, and scared of getting closely involved with somebody in this situation. When the transports begin, each day could be our last."

"Isn't that a good reason to make the most of every day?" he asked.

"On the one hand yes, but I'm afraid of the turmoil it will cause up here." She tapped her forehead.

"Which is why we'd better get on with what we're doing." He smiled and rested his hand on the shoulder of the space suit.

"Let's talk about it again in a quieter moment," whispered Ellen.

"I look forward to it," he whispered back.

She reached for a bundle and handed it to him. "This is the underwear. Its actual name is LCVG."

"LCVG?"

"Yes, it stands for Liquid Cooling and Ventilation Garment. NASA slang. You wear it under the space suit. There are little tubes woven into it that circulate water and air through the suit to regulate the temperature."

Russell disappeared behind a curtain, took off his uniform and squeezed himself into the tight underwear. He was barely able to pull up the zipper. When he was done he presented himself to the expert.

"Well, that looks pretty sexy," Ellen winked.

"At least it's not pink," Russell retorted

laconically.

"Good," she said and briefly checked the fit of his new outfit. "Before getting out of the shuttle you usually breathe pure oxygen for around four hours, in order to purge the nitrogen from your body. The air pressure is lower in the suit than in the space station, otherwise you would end up getting the bends. The nitrogen releases into the bloodstream and forms little gas bubbles, which can cause an embolism. But we'll give all that a miss today and just do a dry run."

"What's this? It looks like a diaper." He held up a white bundle.

"We'll spare ourselves that today, too."

Russell was taken aback. "Are you serious? That was supposed to be a joke."

"Well, we sometimes work for up to eight hours outside the space station and sometimes you have to go." She grinned again. "In NASA slang, the diaper is called a MAG. MAG stands for Maximum Absorbency Garment—and you have no idea how expensive it was to develop."

Russell held the diaper like a dead rat between his thumb and forefinger, before dropping it back on the table. "I don't want to know," he murmured.

Her mouth twitched. "Around three-hundred feet of tubing for water and air are sewn into your underwear, because cooling and ventilation are a big problem in the suit. The tubes in the underwear are connected to the HUT."

"The what?"

"The Hard Upper Torso, the upper part of the space suit to which the PLSS is attached."

"What's that again? You and your acronyms at NASA—I remember it put me on edge when I did those reduced-gravity flights. Whenever one of you NASA people is around, you feel like an idiot. It's part of your strategy, isn't it?" He ended his tirade with a grin.

"Yup. The secret code of the holy brotherhood of astronauts." Ellen grinned back. "PLSS is for Primary Life Support System. The backpack has got tanks inside it for oxygen and water, and there are also batteries, all the electrical equipment, and the monitoring devices. Like a little spaceship, it supplies your suit with everything you need to stay alive."

Russell pulled on the lower part of the white suit of armor. It didn't look that different from a normal pair of pants but it was much heavier. Then he slipped his arms into the upper, hard half. Ellen closed the ring that connected both parts at the waist. The collar of the suit was very high and had a little screen fastened to it, so that Russell could see several displays right in front of him. Ellen plugged in a cable and the screen lit up.

"Here you can read the status of the suit— oxygen supply, pressure, temperature. All there. There is a tube in front of your mouth from which you can drink during the mission. It is fed by the IDB—the In-Suit Drink Bag, which is attached to the HUT." Smiling, she waited for his response.

"Surely you don't expect me to learn all these acronyms. What's this black switch for? I can't even reach it when I've got my helmet on."

Ellen giggled. "That isn't a switch. You can use it to scratch yourself if you get an itchy nose. It's made out of sponge."

"And how on earth did you come up with something like that?"

"When an Apollo astronaut was within an inch of aborting his mission because his itchy nose was driving him to distraction."

Russell rubbed his nose with the soft little stick. "Hmm, feels good. That really was a great idea. What's next?"

"Now you put on your headset—or your CCA for Communications Carrier Assembly, if you can cope with another acronym. Make sure it fits well. You can adjust it with that strap there. I'll plug it into the HUT."

While Russell stood there stiffly, she began adjusting his high-tech cladding.

"Right, great," she said. "Now look down to your chest. The box is for controlling your suit."

"Come on, give me the acronym!"

"DCM. Stands for Displays and Control Module. By turning this you can control the temperature and the coolant inflow. And with the switches here you can turn various subsystems on and off as well as operate the radio device. But we'll practice that another time."

She pointed at various parts of his chest. But the collar was so high and stuck out so stiffly from his body, he couldn't even look down the front of his suit.

"I can't even see the switches," he said. "I can't see anything that's on the front of this thing."

"Look at the left arm of your suit. There's a mirror attached, that will help you."

He lifted his left arm, and sure enough, he could now see everything on his chest. The words on the switches were even written in reverse.

"I have to admit, you guys are pretty smart."

"Well, the Russians are even better. But when they built the Soyuz capsule, nobody tested whether the cosmonauts could reach the switches. They have to take sticks with them to reach some of them!"

Ellen then showed him how to pull on and attach the helmet and the gloves, and explained how to operate the suit. Then Russell had a go alone. He took the EMU on and off without any help, until he felt like he had come to grips with it. Barely a minute later, General Morrow was standing behind him with John Rushworth, to whom Ellen explained the suit next. Russell was soaked in sweat from head to toe, and headed for the shower.

8. The First Transport

Over the following days they familiarized themselves with the equipment they would need for the transport. Morrow kept scheduling practice sessions until Russell could practically operate the suit and the devices in his sleep. After a few days the general called them in for a last-minute meeting, in which he informed them that the first training missions with the teleportation machine would begin the next day. The destination of these missions was the Summers planetoid, and Russell volunteered for the first one. They would be accompanied on the transport by an experienced astronaut. To everyone's surprise it counted as one of their ten missions.

In the morning they drove into the tunnel and down to the cave. Russell retreated to a container, where he spent two hours breathing in pure oxygen from a mask. Colonel Holbrook, who would accompany him on the transport, sat beside him. Because of the masks on their faces they weren't able to talk. When the two hours were up, the men put on their space suits with the help of several technicians, activated all the systems and checked whether everything was functioning properly.

"Good, Russell," praised Holbrook. "You got the hang of using the EMUs pretty quickly. Just a couple of things about today's mission: If you stick by my side and don't do anything stupid, it will all go fine."

"How often have you made this trip?"

"Today is about the thirtieth time. I stopped counting. A lot of missions were needed to set up the base. Let's go."

The two men stomped clumsily out of the container. To Russell the suit felt incredibly heavy, although its weight had been reduced as much as possible. They lumbered over to the sphere, which sat in the dark cave like an exotic object. As they entered the alien machine, Russell noticed the strange headache again—like a switch had been flipped in his head. It felt as if worms were crawling through his brain behind his temples. Although the pain didn't get worse, it was far more severe than a hangover after a hard night of boozing.

The other members of the group were waiting inside the big sphere and watched them full of curiosity. They all knew that they would soon be making this same journey. Ellen nodded at him encouragingly.

Two engineers were standing in front of the control pillar, waiting. Russell trudged up behind Holbrook to the transporter sphere, where an opening had already appeared in the outer wall.

"Go through and close the opening. Just press on any point next to it."

Russell tentatively laid his hand on the wall and wondered what it was made of. It looked as smooth and hard as metal, but when he laid his hands on it, he could feel a slight resistance just above the surface, as if were covered in a layer of invisible foam. After just a few seconds of holding his fingers on the wall, it closed. However, there was no closing mechanism to be seen. From one moment to the next the opening was simply not there anymore. It had closed without making a sound.

"Right, let's check our gear one last time, and then we can go," said Holbrook.

Russell scanned the displays. All the parameters were correct, so he pulled down his visor and opened the oxygen valve on the box on his chest.

"Okay, Russell. Enter the destination combination on the control pillar. Every time you touch it, the current symbol moves forward. Repeat until the desired symbol appears, and then start on the next one."

Russell touched the first symbol. The surface of the control pillar appeared to be made of black glass and resembled a modern touchscreen. A little checklist was attached to the arm of his space suit, including the symbol sequence for his destination. The sequence for his return to Earth was printed below it. Of course they had had to learn this combination by heart during their training, so that the print-out was just a precaution.

After three touches, the first symbol corresponded to the one on his checklist. He continued until all the symbols matched. Holbrook checked the display and gave him the thumbs up.

"Good. Now press on the white field below it."

Russell pressed on it, and another white rectangle appeared to the left.

"And now?"

"Now I wish you luck on your first transport!"

Russell looked at his companion incredulously. "Transport? Does that mean that … Oh."
Only then did he notice the sluggish sensation in his stomach. He reached for his ballpoint pen, which was secured with Velcro next to the checklist, and let it go. The pen floated in front of his face, turning slowly.

"You can't feel the teleportation at all. Incredible!

And in the tight suit you don't notice the weightlessness either."

"We're not completely weightless. The gravitational pull on the planetoid is about a fiftieth of what it is on Earth."

Now Russell could see that the pen was very slowly falling to the ground, as if in slow motion.

"The escape velocity of the planetoid is very low. With a strong leap you can leave its force field. Come on, we'll go outside. Use your thrusters."

Russell tested the thruster system. On various parts of the suit were vernier thrusters, which helped with maneuvering in zero gravity. Using the controls on his chest, he accelerated toward the wall. It all worked without a hitch.

Holbrook made an opening in the wall of the transporter and floated slowly through it. Russell followed him into the bigger sphere.

The outer cavity was the same as the one on Earth. On their expeditions out here, the astronauts had obviously brought all kinds of devices and equipment with them, which were now strewn around everywhere. And there were ropes crisscrossing the sphere.

"The ropes save us time and fuel. Just move your way along the rope behind me as far as the outer wall."

Up to now, Russell had been more-or-less able to ignore the weightlessness. But here in the bigger sphere it was no longer possible. Soon he was floating upside down and twelve feet from the ground of the outer sphere. It was impossible to tell what was up and what was down.

Russell began to feel slightly queasy, but he

remembered the training he had done in similar conditions. He fought the feeling by looking for a fixed point, and choosing one wall as the ground and the other as the ceiling. Then he pulled himself clumsily along the rope. It was difficult to judge his movements correctly, and he kept drifting off to the side.

Holbrook clearly found it easier. With quick, deft movements he pulled himself along the rope and was soon floating next to the outer wall of the sphere. Gasping for breath, Russell finally also reached it. He grinned at the astronaut, who didn't seem to find working in zero gravity the least bit arduous.

"You're in good shape, Holbrook."

"You're right about that. But in the end it's all a matter of experience. Until you've learned to correctly judge your movements, it's really exhausting moving in this kind of environment. Later, once you've had more practice, it's easier than a walk on Earth. You pull on the rope once and immediately float off until you've reached your goal. But if you haven't mastered it yet, you keep drifting off, and then it turns into hard work. It's difficult to manoeuver yourself back into the direction you want to go. But I reckon you're doing pretty well. For one thing, you haven't puked in your helmet like I did on my first space walk."

"Why do you think I didn't have any breakfast?" replied Russell, but he didn't get a response from his companion.

"Watch out, I'm going to open the outer wall now. The station module is about three-hundred feet away. There are ropes outside, too. To be on the safe side, we should hook ourselves to the rope."

Holbrook opened the entrance and pulled

himself through. Russell floated behind him.

"Holy shit."

He was looking at a lunar-like, slightly hilly landscape covered in a gray powdery substance. Everywhere there were little craters. The horizon appeared to be not more than about six-hundred feet away, and up above, a green sun shone in the black sky along with millions of stars. The Milky Way was brighter than he had ever seen it from Earth, and everything was shrouded in an almost unbearable silence.

"I'm starting to understand why you boys love your job so much."

"Now you're also an astronaut, Harris. Congratulations! In the last few minutes you've come further than the Apollo astronauts could ever have dreamed of."

Russell snapped the carabiner around the rope that was attached to the outside of the sphere and tied to poles inserted in the ground at regular intervals. It led to an object about three-hundred feet away that resembled a gray, upturned garbage can. It was affixed to the ground with steel cables.

Holbrook pulled himself along the rope toward the station.

"How did you get that thing here?" asked Russell. "It's too big for the transporter."

"We transported the module in pieces and assembled it here. It's an accommodation module originally intended for the International Space Station, but for financial reasons it wasn't taken there. NASA modified and reequipped it. And the pressurized mating adapter was replaced with an airlock." Holbrook reached the airlock and opened it with a few hand movements. "NASA is already working on a bigger dome that we want to build over the transporter," he continued. "Once we've provided it with the right atmospheric pressure, we can come here without our space suits."

"It's certainly strange that after the transport you're immediately exposed to the destination's atmosphere," Russell mused. "Our air ought to remain in the transporter until the outer wall is opened."

"I presume the air isn't teleported along with the sphere. If you have a chance, you should ask Dr. Gilbert about it. He has his own theories."

"And what do you think, Holbrook?"

"I stopped thinking a long time ago. I would rather admit right away that I have absolutely no idea. Sometimes you get through life more easily with that attitude."

Russell and his companion pulled themselves into the airlock. Then the astronaut closed the door and started the pressure equalization. Seconds later Russell heard a hissing sound, which gradually got louder.

"Pressure equalization completed. You can close the valve on your suit and take off your helmet."

Russell took off his helmet and ran a hand through his hair. It was wet with sweat.

"And now?"

Holbrook opened the inner door and began to take off his space suit. "First we'll have a break, then we'll do some work on the module."

"What are you doing here, actually?"

"Part of the module is an autonomous telescope that systematically scans the sky. We're creating a map of the stars to try to work out the position of this planetoid in the galaxy."

"Isn't it possible that we're in another galaxy?"

"No, we've already identified a few of the other well-known galaxies, like the Andromeda Galaxy. Their positions aren't very different, so we presume that we're no further than twenty-thousand light years away from Earth. But we are definitely further away than a thousand light years."

"How can you know that?"

"Because if we were closer we would be able to see the classic constellations. But we haven't been able to identify them. Now we're trying to find the pulsars of the Milky Way. Every pulsar has its own unique frequency, so they can be precisely identified. Because this frequency changes very slightly over the years, we can draw conclusions about the current time."

"How do you mean?"

Holbrook shrugged. "Who says that the transporter only travels through space?"

"Jesus, you mean that thing is also a time machine?"

The astronaut hesitated. "No, I don't think so. And our physicists don't think so either. But there's no harm in finding out for sure. But above all, we want to know where we are. That might help us understand the significance of the destination selector. It could be that the symbols define a system of coordinates. But to work that out, it's vital to know the position of the Summers planetoid relative to Earth. The pulsars will help us."

Russell didn't even know exactly what pulsars were. However, he didn't want to come across as dumb, so he didn't ask any more questions. He would get Ellen or Albert to explain it to him later.

Holbrook installed various pieces of equipment in the station and saved the latest data recorded by the telescope.

While they were waiting, Russell floated along the wall and kept looking out of the little window at the crater landscape. He thought about the fact that he and Holbrook were the only human beings within a radius of thousands of light years. It made him feel very lonely. What would it be like when he had to make his first trip alone? He pushed the frightening thought to the back of his mind and peered over Holbrook's shoulder. He was busy doing something on a laptop.

"What did you do before this project? Were you on the space station?" asked Russell.

The astronaut typed something into the computer, whereupon the telescope outside turned by one degree. Then he closed the laptop.

"I started out as a space shuttle pilot. When the shuttle program was suspended, I worked for a long time in Houston on the simulator of the Orion capsule. But the program moved so slowly. The more delays there were, the more fed up I got with the Astronaut Office. I turned down a long-term mission to the ISS."

"Why? I would have thought that was every astronaut's dream come true."

"I couldn't get excited about the prospect of spending half a year living in a garbage can in orbit and carrying out experiments that some egghead down on Earth dreamt up. I'm a pilot, not a scientist. The worst thing was that I would have started with a

Russian Soyuz rocket. I couldn't bear the idea of flying as a passenger in a Russian capsule and twiddling my thumbs during takeoff. When the United States threw out its space shuttles, we became reliant on the Russians. But I didn't want to play along with that, either. When I was offered this project I had already announced that I was leaving NASA." Holbrook took a data carrier from the shelf and stuck it into the disk drive. "This is the last one. Then we're done for now."

"It sure is incredible," said Russell. "We're light years away from Earth and we'll still be home in time for supper. What did you think the first time you saw the transporter?"

"I was overwhelmed. It was as if a door to the whole universe had been opened. I'd been suffering from depression for several years, and then it was gone from one moment to the next. My life suddenly had meaning again."

"You don't have any family?"

"No. For me there was never anything except the space program. And now it's too late for all that." The astronaut hesitated a few seconds before continuing: "Also, I don't really think I'm cut out for family life. Doing the school run every morning and hanging out on the porch on Sunday afternoons. Frankly, the idea freaks me out!"

He gazed out of the window.

"Look outside. Isn't it fantastic? An alien world. And only a few of us will ever get to experience such an adventure. I needed this. Normal life on earth bores me to tears."

"I could happily do without the adventure of being teleported to an unknown destination," replied

Russell, a tone of bitterness in his voice.

"Yeah, I know. I'm sure you can imagine how I felt when I discovered what had happened to Captain Summers."

"Of course; and after that, none of your people wanted to select an unknown destination," Russell reminded him.

"Of course not. Astronauts don't shy away from taking risks, otherwise nobody would volunteer to sit on the top of a rocket. But nobody wants to embark on a fatal mission, either. And I want you to know that I was against the forced conscription of prisoners to do this job. But nobody listens to me. At some point we'll get to the bottom of the secret of this transporter."

"It's okay. I can't complain. Without this forced conscription I would already be dead. At least it gives me a chance. —Look, what's that blinking on the console?"

Holbrook turned around. "The backup is finished." He took the data carrier out of the drive and slid it into a silver case. "Our job is done. Let's go home, Harris."

They helped each other into their space suits and then returned to the transporter and back to Earth.

9. The Lottery

Over the following days the others also completed their training missions with the transporter. Michael Bridges was the last of them. He returned together with the astronaut Walter Redmont, and General Morrow announced a meeting for that same evening. Russell could imagine what it was about. It was time for the first transports to unknown destinations. It was getting real now.

General Morrow entered the meeting room with a cool expression. He was followed by the physicist Gilbert, the engineers Blumberg and Aldrich, as well as Dr. Cummings. The astronauts Holbrook and Redmont were the last to enter the room.

Holbrook was carrying a case of beer, and proceeded to hand out cans to everyone in the group. Russell ripped his open and sat down beside Ellen at the big, round table.

After Morrow had sorted through some papers on the table, he stood up and immediately silenced the chatter. He spared himself a preamble.

"Your training is complete and the President has authorized me to begin the exploratory missions. We won't waste any time and will start tomorrow morning. Dr. Gilbert has developed a procedure for the order of the destinations. As I've said before, we hope to quickly decipher the system of the machine. What is important is to identify the position of each destination. For this reason, the first thing you will do after a successful transport is to check out the environmental conditions. If the destination appears to be worthwhile, you will leave the sphere, take some photos of the surroundings and leave behind a probe, which will be collected in a later mission by an experienced astronaut. Further reconnaissance will take place later depending on the data."

"How should we know if a destination is *worthwhile*?" asked Hilmers, who up to now had always kept a low profile, but was increasingly pushing himself to the fore.

"If you survive the transport, it means it's worth returning for a closer look."

There was an outbreak of muttering and General Morrow raised his voice.

"Each of you will soon complete a mission. There will be one mission a day—regardless of what happens. Afterwards, the data will be evaluated and the course of action revised as necessary. Soon after that, the next series of ten missions will start."

"If there are even ten of us still left!" Hilmers said grimly.

"Yes, I'm working on the assumption that all of you will survive your first mission. But don't forget, it's possible that we might find out how the machine works on one of the first trips. Perhaps one of you will come across a base belonging to the aliens, where we can find the necessary information. You still have a fair chance."

O'Brien laughed shrilly before flashing his hate-filled eyes at the general. "And who do you want to stick into the machine from hell first?"

"We've given that some thought. First we wanted you decide amongst yourselves, but I doubted that would work. That's why we've decided on a lottery. Unless somebody wants to volunteer?"

Nobody volunteered. So Morrow took off his peaked cap, took out ten folded pieces of paper from his briefcase and placed them in the hat.

"Everyone takes one piece of paper. They are numbered from one to ten."

He walked around the table. His hands shaking, Russell took out one of the bits of paper, hesitated briefly and then opened it.

At least he wasn't the first.

Ellen whistled through her teeth as she looked at her paper. And when it was O'Brien's turn, he gave another piercing laugh.

General Morrow walked up to the board, on which he drew a table. In the left column he wrote down the names of the candidates, one after the other, drawing a line from top to bottom after the names. A moment later he turned around, looked directly at Russell and adopted his commanding tone of voice.

"Harris?"

Russell threw his piece of paper on the table.

"Four."

The general wrote a four after his name.

"Bridgeman?"

"Five."

"And you, Miss Slayton?"

Russell pricked up his ears.

"Two."

He looked at Ellen in shock. She nodded to him and then shrugged.

Only now was it dawning on him that it was getting serious. *Will I still be alive in a week? Will Ellen still be alive in a week?*

"Hilmers?"

"I've got number eight."

"O'Brien?"

Sean O'Brien was still laughing. He took his piece of paper, scrunched it up and threw it across the table. It landed in front of Morrow, who picked it up.

On the board next to O'Brien's name he wrote down the number one.

10. The Physicist

Russell couldn't sleep. His mind was buzzing. After tossing and turning for nearly two hours, he got up.

He crept down to the rec room and looked out of the window. A light was still burning in the building next to the accommodation block. He saw Dr. Gilbert scurrying past one of the windows. Obviously, the physicist couldn't sleep, either.

He went over to see what the scientist was up to.

In the workshop, Gilbert was fiddling around with a piece of equipment. As Russell approached him from behind, he gave a start.

"Oh, Harris. I didn't hear you coming. What are you doing here?"

Russell laughed. "That's just what I wanted to ask you, Doc."

Gilbert nodded. He showed Russell the component on which he was working. "Here you can see the scanner that O'Brien will take with him tomorrow—I mean, today. It's a little spectrometer for analyzing the destination's atmosphere—if there is one. The instrument only arrived today. It's much more sensitive than the module that was previously built into the scanner. I wanted to install it in order to get better results. I'm glad we're working on discovering the secret of the sphere again."

"You admire the aliens' technology, don't you Doc?"

"Yes, it's the most fascinating technology I've ever come across." The physicist's voice almost cracked with enthusiasm.

"Listening to you, I get the impression there is nothing more important for you in life. Is that true?"

The physicist looked at him earnestly. Finally he sat down on the stool next to him.

"You know, Harris, I've always longed for a project like this. In fact, I've secretly dreamed about it! An alien object whose secrets are within our reach. That is—assuming we're intelligent enough to decipher them."

"You love enigmas, don't you?"

"Yes, the more complicated the better."

Russell nodded. He looked at the gaunt man sitting on his stool: he was exhausted, but the fervor in his eyes was undimmed. Over the years his iron will had created furrows in his face, which only accentuated his determination.

"You know, when I was still young, my parents were always fighting," the scientist continued. "They didn't get on all too well. They were constantly screaming at each other, or at me, and I was punished for things I hadn't done."

Gilbert took off his spectacles and looked out of the window into the night. Russell stood there in silence. He hadn't expected the physicist to talk to him so openly.

"I wasn't too popular at school, either. And when I look at old photographs of myself I can see why. I looked like some kind of weird hawk, my glasses were far too big."

"And then you immersed yourself in science?"

"Yes, science made sense to me, it was so logical. You just had to be intelligent enough to understand the laws of nature. And I understood all the books, I read them in record time. I was particularly fascinated by particle physics because it explains what holds our universe together at its core. I achieved a level of knowledge that nobody around me had. Finally I had something that made me feel superior. When the others pushed me around, I always consoled myself that I had this knowledge and they didn't."

"And that thing down there in the cave?"

Gilbert put his glasses back on. "The transporter is the first machine that has pushed me to my limits. And I've designed compact nuclear reactors for submarines! I didn't find that complicated or even challenging. Almost boring in fact. But that machine down there ... I don't understand anything. I haven't the faintest clue how it works and why it works. It's driving me crazy!"

Russell raised his eyebrows.

"It's driving me nuts! I need to get to the bottom of how it works," Gilbert continued. "I simply have to! Do you understand, Harris?"

Russell shook his head. Up to now he'd thought the physicist was a levelheaded, sensible person. This glimpse behind the façade scared him.

"No, Doc. Not really. But tell me: how do you think it works? Do you have a theory?"

Gilbert shrugged. "I've racked my brains night after night. I have a theory, but I could be completely wrong."

"Do you want to tell me?"

"I doubt you'll understand it. What do you know about the structure of the universe, Harris?"

"Phew, what a question! Well, there are atoms that consist of nuclear particles, and then there are light particles that are flying around everywhere."

Gilbert smiled. "Yes, that's a start, I suppose. I think—and I'm not the only one to do so—that the entire universe is a never-ending, multidimensional matrix."

Russell shook his head doubtfully. "Can we start with quantum physics for dummies?"

Gilbert laughed. He stood up and went over to his computer. Russell followed him. The physicist opened up an image of a smiling woman, then he zoomed in so close that you could see the pixels.

"This picture can be clearly defined with the help of its pixels. These colored pixels here constitute three variables: red, green and blue values. By giving each of these three variables a value, you get a particular color tone."

"I don't understand what you're getting at, Doc. Are you trying to say that the universe consists of individual pixels?"

"Well yes, it's a little more complicated though, as you have to work with probabilities in quantum mechanics, but you can break it down to this basic idea. Quantum physicists even know the size of these minimum quantities of space and time. They result from the Planck constant. You can't infinitely divide a unit of time. In the same way, it doesn't make sense to try and further divide the minimum length unit that Planck defined. If you combine the two, you end up with what I like to call spacetime pixels."

"If you say so ..."

"Yes, I say so, and others say so too! Every pixel in the universe is made up of several variables. These variables stand for the individual fields that are present in the universe: the electromagnetic field, the gravitational field, the field of weak interaction, and so on. The values of the variables determine the strengths of the individual fields."

"And if all the variables are known?"

"Then you've precisely defined space or a section of it."

"That sounds logical, but does it have to do with the transporter?"

"Well, I think the transporter functions on the basis that it can modify, read, or overwrite the multidimensional field in the little sphere—like a computer reads a hard drive and sends the data via the Internet to a computer in Australia or Europe."

"And in terms of the transporter? What is the 'Internet' there?"

"Wormholes!"

"What?"

"Let me elaborate. Have you heard of so-called quantum teleportation?"

"Doesn't that have to do with the transfer of properties to another particle?"

"Yes exactly. Your general knowledge isn't bad, Harris. With quantum teleportation, particles interact in correlation. We say they are *entangled*. Even if you now divide up these particles and place them at a distance of light years from one another, they are still connected to each other. Just like your twin brother has the same blond hair as you."

"And?"

"Now comes the exciting bit. If you dye your hair black, then your entangled twin brother gets black hair too."

"That's crazy!"

Gilbert laughed. "That's what Einstein said about quantum physics. He ridiculed it as *spooky action at a distance*. Can you imagine?"

Russell remained silent.

"But every experiment carried out since then has

confirmed the theory of quantum physics, which results in the possibility of quantum teleportation."

"Doc, I can't keep up. What has that got to do with the transporter? That thing isn't an elementary particle."

"I'm getting to that. In 2013, a team here in the USA started to investigate how quantum teleportation, which results from quantum physics, could be linked to the theory of relativity."

"Listen, Doc. I don't understand these things."

"Wormholes!"

"What?"

"It's assumed that a wormhole is created between two entangled particles, through which they are always connected. And every single space quantum in the inner sphere of the teleportation machine is connected with other inner spheres that are elsewhere in the galaxy; again, through the wormhole. These distant spheres are in turn connected to others—resulting in an absolutely incredible galactic network."

Gilbert was now in full flow. He was practically bursting with excitement. It dawned on Russell that the physicist had fallen in love with the transporter. Not just in the figurative sense. He began to suspect that in some grotesque way, there was an erotic element to his obsession.

"You know, Harris, I also think that the transport process can be intelligently controlled by the sphere. The sphere recognizes if there is a human being inside, and is able to differentiate between the objects inside it. That explains why the atmosphere isn't also transported."

"What do you mean by *intelligent*, Doc?"

"I presume that the transporter is controlled by

some kind of intelligent computer. You know what I mean, an artificial intelligence."

"Well, the transport system with its control pillar and the phone principle doesn't strike me as particularly intelligent."

"No, no, Russell. Do you see this here?" The physicist took a smartphone out of his bag. He pressed a button on the side and the screen lit up. The word Emergency appeared on the screen for making an emergency call. "Give a person who was alive fifty years ago this phone. He'll think that you can only make emergency calls on the phone. He has no idea of everything that is possible with this device once you enter the correct PIN."

"And you think that ..."

"I think that the transporter can be controlled in a very different way and that many other things are possible with the sphere."

"But?"

The physicist's shoulders drooped. "But we're too stupid to understand it. I'm too stupid. I have to get to the bottom of how this thing works. I simply have to, do you understand, Harris?"

Russell returned to the accommodation block. Could it really be? Was there some kind of comprehensive instruction manual for the machine out there, which simply hadn't been found yet? Gilbert seemed to be convinced that this was the case, and was intent on penetrating the secret—no matter what the cost.

He felt his chest tightening with anxiety. He presumed that the physicist would let each and every one of the former prisoners die in the sphere, if it promised him just one more quantum of knowledge about the alien machine.

As Russell approached the door to the sleeping quarters, he heard a noise. Someone was running down the corridor.

Quietly he turned the corner just in time to see the door to O'Brien's room closing and hear the snap of the lock.

But the room to Ellen's room was half open. He looked inside, confused. His comrade was standing in front of her bed in just her underwear, a look of shock on her face.

"Is everything okay?" he asked.

"That was O'Brien! He was suddenly standing in my room!"

Ellen was breathing heavily, and sweating. Russell stepped into the room and closed the door.

"Did he hurt you? What happened?"

Ellen sat down on her bed and turned her puffy eyes to Russell. He sat down beside her and took her hand. She was shaking.

"I woke up suddenly and at first just had a vague feeling that something wasn't right," she began in a choking voice. "Then I heard somebody breathing and saw a shadow in front of my bed. I ... must have forgotten to lock my door. O'Brien ..." with an effort she took a deep breath. "He was standing in front of my bed jerking off. When he saw that I'd woken up, he lay down on top of me."

Russell said nothing. Obviously that lowlife needed his bones broken more than once—although the sphere might take care of the problem far more efficiently.

"Out of a reflex I just rammed my knee where it hurts. He fell off the bed and ran out. I was half asleep through all of it."

Russell could feel another surge of rage well up inside him. "That lousy son-of-a-bitch. He really doesn't know where to stop. I'm going to go and teach him a lesson."

"No," said Ellen. "He's already learnt his lesson. He won't try it again."

"Still. This whole time he's done nothing but cause trouble and drive us nuts. And now this! It can't go on like that. The next time he fucks up, he's won't get away with it."

He tried to calm himself down and breathed deeply.

"Are you okay, Ellen? Shall I stay with you for a while?"

She smiled at him from beneath her mussed up hair. "It's okay, Russell. Go and sleep. I'll be alright."

I know you will, he thought, and crept back to his room.

11. O'Brien

Russell stood a few feet behind the control pillar in the outer sphere. Gilbert and the engineers Blumberg and Aldrich were fiddling around with the controls and talking to each other in animated voices. A little while earlier, the physicist had presented his idea of moving one code symbol by one position each mission. If he could get location data from some of these destinations, he hoped to be able to infer a system.

Several cameras were placed around the inner sphere, as were measuring devices and scanners. General Morrow, some other high-ranking military officials, and two men in suits were also standing to the side, watching the proceedings. One of them was speaking quietly into a Dictaphone.

After entering the alien contraption, Russell was immediately besieged by one of those headaches, which was particularly strong today. He put it down to the beer and the excitement of last night.

O'Brien stepped into the sphere in a space suit. His helmet visor was still open. But his face, which usually had such a violent expression, looked different. Emptier? Or just detached? Russell couldn't quite say, but it was noticeable.

Next to him, Holbrook stepped into the sphere wearing a blue uniform with NASA insignia. Slowly O'Brien approached the steps, then stopped short. He looked at Ellen and whispered something in her ear. Russell saw her eyes widen.

What vulgar things is the prick filling her head with now?

Then O'Brien turned around abruptly and walked past Russell. He stopped in front of him, too.

"I'll see you in hell, Harris!"

After giving a nod, he pulled down his visor and made his way up the steps with a determination one didn't expect from him. With his head raised high, he stepped into the inner sphere without turning around and closed the opening.

Gilbert had a microphone attached to his overall and spoke via the loudspeaker. His words were being recorded.

"Okay. The opening is closed. Transport in sixty seconds." He turned around to the group gathered around the sphere. "After starting the transport, we wait sixty seconds. If he's in danger, O'Brien can return by himself at any time. If he reaches his destination safely he should cut the connection—then we'll know everything is okay. In that case he's expected to go on a recon and return after an hour at most. If the connection hasn't been broken after a minute, and he hasn't returned, we will assume that something has gone wrong. In that case we will start the return transport from here. Another thirty seconds. All clear?" He looked at the engineers.

"All clear, recording devices on," said Blumberg.

Gilbert looked over to Morrow, who gave a curt nod.

"Good," said the physicist and began to count down the seconds: "Ten, nine, eight, seven …" His hand hovered over the field below the destination code. "Three, two, one …" He pressed on the field. "Transport completed." His voice, which had been calm up to now, went up a tone.

Russell could imagine why. Finally the scientist would be gaining new insight into how the sphere worked. And he didn't care about the sacrifices that would have to be made along the way.

"The clock is ticking. Three, four, five, six …"

Russell closed his eyes. It was hard for him to imagine that O'Brien was now light-years away and not inside the gently floating orb. He hoped that he would return in one piece. It would increase his chances too.

He opened his eyes and looked at the control device. Tensely he waited for the fields under the code to disappear. It would mean that O'Brien had cut the connection and therefore reached his destination safely.

"Thirty seconds. Another half a minute."

Russell looked over to Ellen. She looked apprehensive, which he could understand only too well. She was the next person to climb into the sphere. Tomorrow, in fact. Regardless of what happened.

"Forty seconds. There's still a connection."

Russell stared at the control pillar, as if he could force it telepathically to cut the connection.

Maybe O'Brien just wants to scare us and is deliberately waiting for them to transport him back.

"Fifty seconds. Return transport in ten, nine, eight …"

The two fields beneath the symbol code disappeared.

"He's transported himself back." Gilbert sounded slightly flustered.

Russell's heart leapt.

He's alive. Thank God.

He heard several of the men around him heaving sighs of relief. The engineer Aldrich smiled, took a video camera from a tripod and directed it at the sphere. The manager next to Morrow gabbled excitedly into his Dictaphone.

The entrance to the inner sphere opened. Out of it came … Russell closed his eyes tightly.

Is that human?

The man next to the general gave a cry of horror into his Dictaphone. The camera fell out of Aldrich's hand and smashed to the floor. Even Dr. Gilbert stepped back in shock.

Out of the opening crawled a strange, steaming, hissing, human-like thing. It must be O'Brien. The remains of his space suit hung from his frame. A terrible stench reached Russell's nose.

My God! What happened to him?

O'Brien hardly resembled a person anymore. His arms and legs had … melted away?

Shreds of dripping white goo stuck to his elbows. As the drops fell to the ground, they dissolved the metal of the steps with a hissing sound. The worst thing was that the thing was still alive. With an unbearable smacking noise it moved forward like a snake and slid grotesquely down the steps. The torso left a trail of slime behind it, which dragged along bits of the space suit.

With agonizing movements, O'Brien crawled toward Russell, leaving a reddish trail of slime behind him. The helmet had dissolved and had melded with the skin of O'Brien's head. Pieces of Plexiglas and thin tufts of hair jutted from the skull, bits of bare bone were visible in several places. His cheeks had dissolved and his entire jaw was exposed up to the nose, which was just a shapeless lump.

Jesus Christ, how could this thing still be alive?

With a silent scream, O'Brien raised his head. His

eye sockets were filled with a pulpy mass, which slowly rolled down his cheeks as white tears. These gruesome eyes looked at Russell for several excruciating seconds. Then they closed forever.

12. Ellen

Russell sat on the bed next to Ellen. She was crying. "Tomorrow could go completely differently," he comforted her.

He dabbed away the tears from her face with a tissue.

In the afternoon there had been a short meeting. Dr. Cummings had presented the results of his first analysis, but the measuring devices on O'Brien's space suit hadn't provided any information. Most of them were completely melted. The doctor had found sulfurous remains on the body, which he had analyzed more closely. He presumed that O'Brien had materialized in an atmosphere consisting of sulfuric acid. From the damage done to the equipment, Gilbert also presumed that the atmospheric pressure must have been very high. That, in turn, had strongly accelerated the decomposition. He expressed surprise that O'Brien had still been able to initiate the return transport. However, the event had not dissuaded the government from pursuing its plan. After a phone call with the Pentagon, General Morrow confirmed that the transports would go ahead over the coming days. Now it was Ellen's turn.

"O'Brien was a shit, but he didn't deserve to go like that," said Russell. "What did he tell you before he went into the sphere?"

Ellen shook her head. "He didn't offend me. On the contrary. He apologized."

Russell looked at her in surprise.

"He said: *I know that I'm an asshole. I put everyone down so that people don't notice that I'm scared. I've always been scared. But not today. Today I don't want to be scared. And that's why I want to tell you something: I'm sorry! And then he went into the transporter.*"

Russell felt nauseous.

Ellen took his hand. "Today I want to tell you what I did."

"You don't have to if you don't want to."

"But I do want to. I don't know what will happen tomorrow, and I see this as a final confession. It's something I'm ashamed of. Eternally ashamed." She looked him in the eyes. "I killed a man."

Russell swallowed.

"We got to know each other at a party in college. It should have been a one-night stand, but six months later we were married. I went to university and made a career for myself at NASA. He had already fought depression during his studies, but somehow he managed to graduate. But then his depression turned into schizophrenia, which he refused to have treated. He couldn't get a job. An acquaintance of mine was a psychologist and he advised me to have him hospitalized. I didn't have the heart to do that, so my acquaintance slipped me the meds under the table. Somehow it went on like that for several years. But when I returned from my last mission, Steve seemed totally changed. He had stopped taking the medication and fallen into a severe psychosis. For days he would sit in a darkened room and brood. He believed that I had been taken over by aliens in space and had returned to kill him. Then one day, he came at me with a knife. I shot him with the pistol that I kept hidden in the apartment."

"But that was self-defense. You were just protecting yourself."

"The judge didn't see it like that. He thought I'd invented the story to get my hands on Steve's family fortune. After all, nobody knew about his illness. And you can't prove that a dead person was psychotic."

"And your acquaintance who provided you with the medication?"

"He swore under oath that he knew nothing. He didn't want to lose his license. Besides, we lived very reclusively. The witnesses who testified in court knew Steve as a quirky but otherwise completely respectable man. I myself contributed to creating the image of an intact family."

"But you're innocent!"

"No, even I don't see it like that. I killed my husband!"

"He attacked you!"

"Because he was ill. It wasn't his fault. I shouldn't have left him alone with his illness. I was selfish; my career was more important to me than he was. I abandoned him and that's why he's dead. It was my fault! And tomorrow I'll pay for it."

Russell didn't know what to say.

"I want to ask something of you," said Ellen.

"Of course."

"Stay with me tonight. I don't want to be alone."

The following morning they waited in the outer sphere for Ellen to appear in her space suit. General Morrow stood to the side and observed the goings-on—this time without the man in the suit. Gilbert and Blumberg stood next to the control pillar. The combination for Ellen's destination had already been entered. Engineer Aldrich was no longer present. After yesterday's events he had asked for a transfer. Instead, another engineer whom Russell didn't know ran from machine to machine checking the configurations.

Russell cursed the damn headaches, which started again as soon as he entered the outer sphere. At least today it wasn't as strong as yesterday. He still had the scent of Ellen's hair in his nose. During the night they had done nothing more than lie beside each other on the bed, but for him it was the sweetest thing he had experienced in many years. He couldn't bear the idea that Ellen was about to climb into the transporter.

Accompanied by Colonel Holbrook, the astronaut entered the sphere. She lumbered over to Russell. The visor was open and she smiled. A tear ran down her flushed cheek. "Thank you for being in my life," she whispered in a scarcely audible voice.

"We'll see each other shortly," he said in a faltering voice.

"Actually it's what I always wanted to do: discover other worlds." She smiled at him again and closed the visor. Then she went up the steps and disappeared into the sphere.

After Ellen had closed the opening, Russell went over to Dr. Gilbert and looked over his shoulder. The physicist began the countdown. Today there was noticeably less euphoria in his voice than yesterday.

"Transport in three, two, one … Completed. The clock is running. One minute."

Russell closed his eyes and wondered whether he should leave the sphere. To witness something like yesterday with Ellen … he wouldn't be able to bear it. Instinctively he counted the seconds, too.

"Seven, eight, nine …"

Please, please.

"Ten, eleven, twelve …"

The fields on the control pillar disappeared and

the code went back to the standard combination. "She cut off the connection. She's alive!"

The relief was palpable. Russell gasped for air. He had been holding his breath without realizing it.

Gilbert turned to him. "I know that you like her. And I'm convinced that she's okay. She cut off the connection to explore the environment."

"I wish I could share your optimism, Doc. We don't know anything about the destination or what dangers await her when she opens the outer sphere."

"We have to be patient. She has an hour before she has to return."

The minutes dragged. Nobody had anything to do. They could only wait. Russell started to talk with the physicist again to distract himself from his oppressive thoughts.

"What happens if someone went into the sphere now and Ellen wanted to return?"

"We carried out that experiment. It doesn't work. Your girlfriend wouldn't be able to transport herself back if somebody else were in the sphere or if the sphere was open."

"And what happens if you open the sphere after the transport is complete, but there's still a connection? Could you get to Ellen?"

"We tried that too. In that case, we can't make an opening." He hesitated. "I think that the transport sphere creates its own universe as soon as it is closed. Like a little bubble that is connected to other parts of our universe by just a few microscopic wormholes. The shell of the transporter separates one universe from the other. Have you heard of the Casimir effect?"

"No Doc. Never heard of it."

"It doesn't matter. Theoretically, you can create another vacuum energy level in a region of space with this effect. Our alien constructors must have put this theory into practice."

Russell shook his head. He didn't understand any of the physicist's theories anymore. He wondered how many centuries ahead of human beings the builders of this strange sphere were. And who they were. Did they live somewhere out there in the galaxy? Or had their civilization been wiped out long ago?

On the control pillar, the combination suddenly changed and a field appeared beneath it.

"She's back!" cried Gilbert excitedly.

The entrance of the inner sphere opened and Ellen came out. She pushed up her visor and winked at the men. They cheered as she came slowly down the steps. Even General Morrow clapped his hands discreetly.

Gilbert ran toward her and ripped the analysis device from her fingers—like a little boy whose mother had brought him a new toy.

Russell hugged her. The other men just stood around her and bombarded her with questions.

"It was incredibly beautiful," she gushed.

"Where were you?"

"After the transport I noticed immediately that the gravitational force was lower. Perhaps a quarter Earth's gravity. The scanner showed an atmosphere. Mainly carbon dioxide like on Mars, but the pressure was higher. I cut the connection to have a look around. It was a red rocky landscape, almost like the pictures of Mars, but with a deep blue, almost black, sky. And up above hung an enormous planet that was shrouded in swirls of cloud like Jupiter. It took up almost the entire sky and was surrounded by a huge ring system. Like Saturn. I've never seen anything more sublime in my life." She smiled and a tear rolled down her cheek. "I took photos, and then carried out the most important analyses. I left the scanner there. Then I got back in the sphere and returned."

Colonel Holbrook listened, open-mouthed. In a few days he would travel to this planet himself, in order to retrieve the scanner and whatever it had recorded.

Meanwhile, the engineer Blumberg had opened a bottle of bubbly, which he now passed around the group. Russell laughed for joy. The day had given him back a bit of hope.

Russell, Ellen, Albert, and Jim gathered in Albert's room. Russell opened another can of beer, while Ellen nipped every now and then at her glass of bubbly. Somehow Albert had managed to requisition a bottle of whisky and was already visibly tipsy. "We always toasted with this stuff after successful SR-71 missions. Good whisky is the only real stuff!"

"I'll stick to beer," said Russell. "It doesn't knock you out as quickly."

"Oh, who cares. That's part of the fun," answered Albert and took another big swig.

Jim had a can of beer in front of him, but didn't drink anything. He found it embarrassing, but he couldn't tolerate alcohol.

"What did it feel like?" he asked Ellen. "I mean in the transporter, just before you started?"

Ellen, who had just been laughing, became serious. She considered for a moment before answering.

"It reminded me of my launches with the space shuttle. You lie on your back in the cockpit of the shuttle and can't do anything at all. You keep looking at the clock that is slowly ticking the countdown. You don't think about the fact that you're sitting on a hydrogen tank with the energy of an atomic bomb and that it could explode at any moment. You forbid yourself to go there. But you also don't think of anything beyond the flight. Astronauts have a saying: No plans beyond MECO."

"MECO?"

"Main Engine Cut-Off. After arriving in orbit. The saying is a relic of the early days of the space shuttle. Back then, several engines exploded on the test-stand and the astronauts flew off in the knowledge that the blades of a ruptured turbo-pump could perforate the hydrogen tank at any moment. That would have destroyed the entire shuttle and you would have died in an instant. The eight minutes from lift-off into orbit feel like being stuck in the narrow neck of an hourglass. You have to get through it. Once you've survived that you suddenly start thinking about things in the future. But not beforehand. When you step into the transporter it's a very similar feeling—only that the chances of surviving are much slimmer."

"How high were the chances in the shuttle?"

"Out of 135 flights, two failed—Challenger and Columbia. In other words, the chances stood at about one to seventy. And if you consider that some astronauts made six or more flights, the chances that they might die went up over course of their careers."

"It's amazing that anybody goes on more than one flight," said Jim.

"You can become really addicted. The thrill of a successful launch, when you're suddenly hanging weightlessly in your seat after the engines have been turned off—it's indescribable." She took a big gulp from her glass. "I got a similar thrill this morning when the transport started and I realized I was still alive."

"The chances have increased a bit again," said Russell. "Four dialed destinations with two losses, means one in two. We're back to where we were two days ago. But the stupid thing is that O'Brien was right. If we don't make a relevant discovery soon, none of us will survive our ten missions."

"We could ask the general if he might consider reducing the number of missions to give us a chance," suggested Jim.

"The general might give it some thought, but President Bigby is the one who decides. He likes to come across as the tough guy. So the probability is exactly zero," said Russell.

"Then we have to get to the bottom of this secret somehow," said Albert.

"But how?" asked Ellen.

Albert shrugged.

"If anybody has an idea, then it's our resident geek," grunted Russell.

"Gilbert? He doesn't seem to have a clue himself," said Albert.

"The guy has a few interesting ideas," explained Russell and shifted in his seat. "I wouldn't be surprised if he could work out a system from the data we're getting."

His friend shook his head. "I reckon scientists like him can't see the forest for the trees."

"What do you mean?"

"For them, everything revolves around the question of how the thing works. But they ought to also be asking themselves how the thing even got here. Did an alien spaceship leave it here? Why was the sphere found at the bottom of the ocean? Whoever put it there must have done so for a reason. I mean, the aliens must have found Earth interesting enough to put a transporter here."

"That sounds logical, but then why did they also put a transporter on that bleak planetoid?" Russell countered. "Or on that hellish planet that got O'Brien? And putting a transporter on a neutron star doesn't make any sense at all."

"In any case, the transporters must be incredibly robust if they can function in environments like that. I wonder how many of those things there are in the galaxy."

Ellen looked up at the ceiling thoughtfully.

"Judging by the number of possible destination combinations, more than a trillion planets would be possible," said Albert.

Jim groaned. "There aren't enough humans on earth to send to their deaths in the transporter."

They carried on speculating for a while, but found themselves going round in circles. At some point Russell went to bed and fell into a fitful, dreamless sleep.

13. Walker

Up to now, Russell hadn't had much to do with Walker. The former soldier was a placid type, who didn't usually push himself to the fore. He was neither particularly likeable nor particularly talkative. He was similar in character to George Williams, Jim's former colleague. So Russell wasn't surprised that the two of them had become friends. Walker nodded to Williams, then put down his visor and disappeared into the sphere.

Gilbert started the transport and began to count down the minute. When the connection broke off, the men clapped. Walker had obviously survived the transport and was now taking a look around. Russell felt a surge of hope. He was earmarked for the next mission, and his chances were improving with each successful trip. Perhaps Walker would even come across some clues and solve the secret of the transporter. It wasn't impossible, but also not very probable.

Walker returned after almost an hour. He stepped out of the transporter, tipped up his visor and laughed triumphantly. Slowly he climbed down the steps, but halfway down he stopped and began to speak in a dramatic tone of voice.

"I was on a small planet, a lot like Summers', but with a spectacular sky. An enormous cloud of stars from horizon to horizon." He was very red in the face.

Too red for a little overexertion, thought Russell.

Walker came down the remaining steps and almost tripped. He had to grip onto the railing.

"What's the matter?" asked Gilbert, walking

toward him.

"I'm a bit dizzy and feel a bit sick. Probably the excitement."

Suddenly engineer Blumberg began to scream.

"Stop! Get away from him!"

Walker blinked in irritation and Gilbert turned round crossly. "What's the problem?"

"My Geiger counter is swinging off the scale. Did you check the radiation levels where you were?"

Walker turned pale. "I didn't think about that."

Gilbert stepped back cautiously.

Walker fell to his knees and vomited, although most of it ran into his space suit.

"Your nausea is the first sign of radiation poisoning, for God's sake!" yelled Blumberg.

Dr. Cummings ran to a cupboard and got out a radiation suit. Together with another paramedic he carried the now unconscious Walker out of the sphere.

"The cloud that the man saw in the sky was probably the remains of a supernova. The planetoid's sun must have exploded and the released neutrons turned the solar system into a radioactive hell," explained Gilbert while reading Walker's scanner. His eyes became wide. "He got over fifty sieverts!"

"What does that mean?" asked General Morrow, who had come up to him.

"That means the man is dead. And you know what's really tragic about it?"

Morrow didn't reply.

"If Walker had read his scanner and come straight back, he would have been okay."

14. Russell

Russell lay beside Ellen on the bed and stroked her hair. "I know that you already heard my story from Jim, but I'd like to tell it to you in my own words, too."

Ellen nodded.

"I've never liked talking about it. Hated to, in fact. Those agonizing days in court; the trial. Just thinking about it was enough to send me over the edge." He paused. "Today it's different. You called it a confession. Perhaps that's a good word. When you know that you might die tomorrow, you want to put everything in order—even if that just means being honest about your own life for once."

"It involves your wife," said Ellen.

"Yes. We met when we were very young. We were never the love of each other's lives, but it worked. Our feelings for each other grew over time, because we knew we could rely on one another— particularly when I was on missions abroad. When I left for Afghanistan, Karen was pregnant. That mission in the Hindu Kush was the worst I had ever been on. We thought we were helping the country, but today I wonder how our politicians could have sent us to that hellhole. I remember every detail about the drive from Kabul Airport into the city, how a little boy used his forefinger and thumb to make the shape of a gun and aimed it at me. It was an omen of what awaited us over the next nine months. I thought we were coming as liberators, but everyone saw us as occupying forces. You never knew who might blow you up the next day or who wanted to shoot you down. There were two things that kept me going through it all: one was the camaraderie in our unit, the other was my family—knowing I could return to them and live my life in peace. You know the rest. So the day I returned to the States turned out to be the happiest and most tragic day of my life."

Ellen just nodded.

"My wife wanted to pick me up at the airport with my little son, whom I hadn't met yet. When I came out of immigration, I looked around for her. Nobody there. Instead a cop approached me and told me to come with him. In a bare little back room of that goddam airport I discovered that my wife and son had been killed in a car crash. They were run over by a drunken truck driver on their way to the airport—and the guy had good connections. He was the brother-in-law of Senator Gould, who later advocated personally for my execution. The guy was released on bail that same evening. I got hold of a gun and found out his address. Then I drove to his place and shot him in the face."

"Do you regret what you did?" asked Ellen.

"Yes. There is nothing in my life that I am more ashamed of."

"It was a kneejerk reaction. The guy killed your family. Your rage was understandable. You shouldn't be too hard on yourself."

"The guy didn't kill them on purpose. Of course he shouldn't have been drunk driving, but he didn't deliberately drive into my wife's car. I, on the other hand, charged straight to his place and shot him in the face, fully aware of what I was doing. It was my decision. Nothing can excuse it and nothing can put it right. And if I take a trip to hell in that damn sphere tomorrow, then I've deserved it."

He turned on his side, with his face to the wall, so that Ellen wouldn't see him crying. She snuggled up to him from behind and at some point he drifted off into a restless sleep.

At six a.m. there was a knock at Russell's door. It was Colonel Holbrook. Ellen had already left an hour ago.

"Russell, are you ready?"

Is today going to be the day I die?

In Afghanistan he had never had those thoughts—even before the most terrible missions. But that thing down there in the cave was something else altogether.

"Yes. We can go, Colonel."

"Call me Christian."

Together they went out, got into the Jeep and drove to the tunnel. Dawn was breaking and on the horizon Russell could see ribbons of orange light. Up above, the sky was still deep black and thanks to the dry desert air you could see millions of stars.

To which of those stars will I be travelling today?

Even if this mission killed him, the idea of traveling to the stars filled him with pride. What would Karen have said if she had been here today? He was overcome by a feeling of calm.

I don't want to die, he thought. *But if that's my fate, I'm going to die with dignity.*

They drove into the tunnel and came to the entrance of the cave. A guard opened the heavy gate and Holbrook parked the Jeep next to a big container. They walked in, side by side. Holbrook helped him into his space suit and together they checked the systems. Then Russell sat down in an armchair, pulled on a mask and breathed in pure oxygen for two hours. During this time he was unable to talk and a thousand thoughts raced through his mind.

Thinking back, memories he had blocked out over the last few months rose unbidden to the surface. He realized that his life hadn't been so bad. He had often complained about his distant parents, but at least they had never maltreated him and had let him do his thing. As a soldier, he had been involved in many terrible things, but at least he had experienced something in his life.

He remembered many of his former friends from Asheville who had never left the place. And he'd had a great wife. Although they'd had their highs and lows, he remembered his years with her as happy ones. And the most important thing was that he had always known that Karen had loved him and that he could trust her. The people he had killed in battle had been fighters themselves; they knew what war meant. He had never let out his frustration on civilians like other assholes in his unit. Once again, he regretted having murdered the senator's brother-in-law. Even if the guy was responsible for the death of his family, it hadn't been right to kill him. Karen would have felt only contempt for that kind of revenge. Which is why, since then, he had also despised himself. He realized that he saw this mission, here and today, as penance. If he died, then so be it. If he survived and made it through this whole thing unscathed, he would do something positive with the rest of his life.

The two hours were up.

Russell closed the valve on the mask and put it on the table. Then he stood up, took his helmet, and left the container. Holbrook accompanied him to the sphere. Soldiers, technicians, and engineers were standing around; as Russell entered, he was met by a range of expressions. He forced a smile, and gave a brief wave. One of the soldiers saluted him. Like in the old days.

Elite soldier Harris makes his way to the helicopter to be flown to enemy territory.

He could feel the tension dissolving, as it so often had in the past when things began in earnest.

Holbrook opened the outer sphere and Russell stepped inside. He stopped for a moment to take in his surroundings. To his left stood General Morrow with two high-ranking officers. Morrow looked at him, and although his expression was impassive, he could see in the general's eyes that this wasn't easy for him either.

To his right were his seven remaining comrades, staring at him with a range of expressions. Ellen stood at the front and smiled. A tear ran down her cheek.

Gilbert and Blumberg were fiddling at the control panel in their white overalls. They were setting the destination and also briefly looked up at him. Due to his talks with Gilbert, something of a friendship had developed between them. He could see that the physicist was tense and didn't feel comfortable in his role today. Blumberg gave a brief nod.

Dr. Cummings was standing in the background with two paramedics who were whispering and glancing at him furtively. He knew exactly what they were thinking: Walker was still lying in hospital, and nobody knew how long he would survive.

Finally he looked at Holbrook, who stood next to him and reached out his hand. Russell took it.

"Have a safe trip. Come back to us."

Finally he went to Ellen. For a long time they looked each other in the eyes, then Russell gave her a gentle kiss on the forehead and turned round to the transporter. The thing hovered in the middle of the room like a black pearl, like a living being that was waiting to devour him, sinister and frightening. A foreign body that didn't belong in this world.

He stepped forward, compared the time on his watch with Gilbert's, and walked purposefully up the steps. At the top, he turned around a last time and waved, then he pulled down his visor. With a dry mouth he stepped through the opening of the sphere and closed it from the inside.

Russell breathed deeply. After a few seconds he looked at his watch. Two more minutes until Gilbert would start the transport. The monitoring devices had already been activated by the technicians, only the portable scanner beside him still needed to be turned on. Russell checked that it was working properly. He wasn't going to let what happened to poor Walker happen to him. But if he ended up on a planet where the gravitational force or the pressure was too high, he wouldn't stand a chance anyway. In that case he wouldn't even be aware of dying.

He stood next to the control pillar. It might be vital for his survival to immediately activate his return transport at the slightest sign of danger.

Thirty seconds.

He breathed calmly. He tried to relax and to suppress the thought of what was about to happen to him. He felt as if his whole life had been headed toward this moment.

Ten more seconds. Nine. Eight. Seven.

Russell closed his eyes and counted the seconds in his head. All he could think of now were these last few numbers before the big zero. He blocked out every other thought from his head.

Four.

Three.

Two.

One.

Zero.

I'm alive!

He emerged on the other side with this one thought.

I'm alive!

He opened his eyes and noticed how not only his heart, but also his stomach, was lurching. It was a familiar feeling.

I'm weightless.

He pulled his legs up and floated in midair.

Air?

He looked at the scanner. No pressure. No atmosphere. No air. No radiation. Nothing obviously dangerous.

He rejoiced inside. At least he would survive this mission.

He turned to the control pillar and pressed on the field that broke off the connection. That way they would know on Earth that he was okay and that he would now set out to explore his surroundings. Walker had also made it this far.

Is there anything I could have overlooked?

It didn't matter. He was here now and decided to make the best of it. Probably he was on some little planetoid again in the depths of outer space. That meant he ought to be able to see the stars outside and photograph them.

Feeling mildly curious, he grasped the rope that was attached to the control pillar, and hooked it to the mechanism on his suit. Dr. Gilbert had attached a motor to the suit, so that when you came back you didn't have to pull yourself laboriously along the rope, but could simply press a button and were pulled back in. The thing worked even if the gravitational force was two times as strong as on Earth, and replaced the unwieldy collapsible ladder they used to have with them to get back into the inner sphere.

Russell floated over to the wall and made an opening with his hand. He had now learned to move around with more agility in zero gravity. He floated elegantly through the opening into the outer cavity, which was completely empty except for the control pillar. Only the strange gray light of the outer wall gave his eyes something to focus on.

Russell slowly left the inner sphere, and got a shock as he suddenly accelerated. Something was pulling him toward the outer wall, which had suddenly turned into a floor, and the force was getting stronger all the time. He sped up until he reached a speed resembling free-fall on Earth. He smashed against the outer wall of the sphere head first with this helmet. In his shock he hadn't found a chance to grasp onto the rope. He somersaulted and landed on his stomach. The palm of his right hand slapped against the wall—in the same way that he touched it when he wanted to open the sphere.

NO!

A gaping hole appeared beneath him and Russell fell out of the sphere into the darkness.

He was seized by panic and could feel the

adrenalin pumping through his body. He clung to the rope in terror, but the motor mechanism locked. He was tossed around by the rope and came to a sudden standstill.

Now the sphere was floating several feet above him. Beneath him was never-ending darkness, and he dangled helplessly from the rope. The rope was the only thing stopping him from falling into that horrendous nothingness below him.

Russell realized that he was safe for the moment. With the motor he could heave himself back into the sphere.

But why was the transporter floating over this nothingness? In the inner sphere he had still been weightless, and now this darkness was trying to pull him into its abyss.

Only now did Russell notice the stars. They rose out of the darkness below him and zoomed at breakneck speed across the "sky." They left streaks on Russell's retina in a ghostly, dark-blue color and raced back toward the darkness on the other side of the sky. They didn't just disappear into the darkness. They merged with a thin ring of blue light that surrounded the vast black area beneath his feet like an aura.

Russell fumbled for the mechanism on his chest and flipped the switch. Slowly he was pulled back up to the opening of the sphere. As he moved toward the sphere, he looked again at the strange sheet lightning on the horizon, which merged with the stars. It was as if the stars were dividing out of fear of the darkness and then gliding around the black nothingness in the form of a ring before reappearing a few seconds later on the other side.

Russell hoped that the helmet camera was working. He didn't even try to take any photos. He wanted to get out of here as quickly as possible. Never before had he felt himself to be in such danger. This wasn't a place for a human being. Forces were at work that transcended the power of the imagination.

Finally he was back in the outer cavity of the sphere and stretched out his hand to close the opening. The moment the opening disappeared he felt a violent vibration from the mechanism on his chest. The cable was jammed, sparks flew out of the housing.

Holy shit.

Russell stood on the floor of the outer sphere to take the pressure off the cable. He pressed on the switched again but the motor was dead.

Shit, shit. Without the motor I can't get back up to the inner sphere!

He quickly pulled out his toolbox from the pant pocket of his suit and yanked opened the housing on his chest. The pulley was broken in three places. He wouldn't be able to pull himself anywhere anymore with this thing. He hooked the rope out of the mechanism and dropped the end down to the floor.

That's it. It's over.

He looked at his scanner. A little more than two pounds. On Earth he would probably have managed to pull himself up the rope, but here in his heavy space suit? No chance.

About ten feet separated him from a safe return to Earth. But it might as well have been ten miles.

Russell looked at the display on his suit. He had enough oxygen left for thirty minutes, then he would suffocate to death.

He summoned all his strength and pulled on the rope. And again. And again. Without success. He wondered whether he could remove the back part of the suit to reduce his weight, but that wouldn't be enough. He would suffocate long before he had managed to pull himself back up.

Exhausted, he floated to the ground.

No chance.

For a moment he thought that the others might send help. Somebody with a rope with which he could be heaved back up. But he immediately dismissed that thought. The opening in the sphere was still there, which meant that this destination couldn't be dialed from Earth. And in any case, the others would assume that he was dead, and nobody would risk selecting this destination again.

Is this it? Am I going to die here in this crazy place?

He could feel tears running down his cheeks.

I would love to see Ellen again!

For a moment, Russell thought about opening the entrance and letting himself fall into the mysterious darkness out there—in the hope of a last, spectacular adventure. But he knew that he wouldn't be able to go through with that.

He imagined Ellen's smile and closed his eyes. He hoped to at least fall asleep forever with this final, pleasant thought.

Abandoning himself to his fate, he tried to put his hand in front of the visor to block out everything around him, but his arm got entangled in the rope. In a final fit of rage he took the rope and hurled it up and away.

His eyes widened. The rope didn't fall back down but floated elegantly past the little sphere. Then it sped up and descended again on the other side of the sphere.

Jesus. What's up and what's down? Somehow everything seems to fall away from the little sphere and somewhere onto the outer wall. But hang on. Does it really?

Russell took his toolbox and flung it toward the outer wall around halfway up the sphere. It slowed down and stopped at the wall.

This is the bottom, but the opposite side is also the bottom. In the middle there's a low gravitational force or else this area is weightless! For whatever reason. So I need to somehow get to the height of the inner sphere. Then maybe I can float over to it.

Russell scrambled up the outer wall. The gloves of his space suit were constantly in danger of sliding off the smooth surface, but he noticed that the force pulling him downward was diminishing. He now crawled on all fours and hoped that the lower gravity would compensate for the steeper wall of the sphere higher up.

It worked. Painstakingly he moved up, and when he was level with the transport sphere he was able to propel himself with the jets on the suit. He steered toward the entrance to the inner sphere. Within a few seconds he had got through the opening.

He took a deep breath.

Jesus, he could have perished. These destinations are far more dangerous than we think.

With a touch of the hand he closed the entrance, floated to the control pillar and entered the code for his return to Earth. Then he looked at the display in front of his neck. He had used up all the oxygen. All he had left was what was circulating in his suit. It didn't matter, in a few seconds he would be back home.

He looked at his watch. His mission had lasted one-and-a-half hours. Half an hour longer than planned. No doubt the others would have written him off.

To hell with it. He was happy to be returning at all.

After taking a deep breath he touched the field on the control pillar.

He could feel gravity returning and pulling him back to the floor of the sphere. He landed with a soft bounce. It was a more familiar pull than the strange gravitational force in that strange place just now. He felt like he was back home.

He didn't even check the scanner, but immediately opened the latch of the helmet, took it off, and breathed deeply.

Survived!

He stumbled on trembling legs to the wall, made an opening and stepped out. There was nobody there. There was nobody anymore in the outer sphere.

Why? Had they really already given up on him?

He hurried down the steps and made an opening into the cave. Some soldiers were working in the background on a scaffold. One of them looked over to him, started to scream and pointed in his direction.

"Over there! Over there!"

The soldiers stopped what they were doing and gawked at him like he was a ghost. General Morrow and Dr. Gilbert stepped out of one of the containers. Morrow gaped at him and the physicist stared at him open-mouthed. They hurried toward him.

"You're alive?" asked Morrow in disbelief.

"We gave up waiting over ten hours ago. We'd

written you off for dead," admitted Gilbert.

Russell shook his head.

Ten hours?

"That can't be, I was only gone for an hour-and-a-half."

Gilbert took the scanner out of his hand and examined him. General Morrow looked at him impatiently.

The physicist looked up in amazement and scrutinized Russell with big eyes before turning to the general. "What he says is true. The device has recorded data points for about one-and-a-half hours. Where the hell were you, Harris?"

Russell told them about the gravitational force that had unexpectedly pulled him to the outer wall, and of the eerie darkness outside the sphere. When he described the stars that had sped across the sky, Gilbert's eyes practically popped out of his head.

"A black hole. That's what it must have been. It explains everything. You were in the orbit of a black hole. Just above the event horizon."

Russell went pale. "A black hole?" And it tried to suck me in?"

"No, it's not as simple as that. The strange force that you felt was the result of the gravity gradients."

"The what?"

"When you floated from the transporter's center of gravity to the outer wall, you were suddenly in a different orbit. The curvature of space close to the event horizon means that within a space of several feet you are already travelling on another orbital path and need a different orbital speed. If you can't change speed, you fall. And this force pulled at you and gave you the feeling of gravity on the rope."

"Yes, but if the rope had ripped, it would have sucked me down into the darkness, wouldn't it?"

"No, Russell. If the rope had ripped, you would simply have floated around the black hole on another orbit. First it would have pulled you down and then into an elliptical orbit. But you wouldn't have fallen in. At least not anytime soon."

Russell shook his head. This was too complicated for him.

"When you climbed up the wall in the sphere, you neared the orbital level of the sphere's center of gravity and had the same orbital speed as the transporter's center of gravity."

"So everything that's on a level with the epicenter becomes weightless? Is that what you're trying to say?"

"That's it, Russell."

"And why did the stars race so quickly across the sky?"

"The sphere was obviously in a stable orbit around the black hole. The gravitational force close to an event horizon is so powerful that the orbital speed is almost as fast as the speed of light. You circled the black hole in the space of a few seconds, which explains the speeding stars. In fact, it was you who was speeding around the black hole." Gilbert stopped to consider for a moment. "It makes sense. The blueshift of the stars also suggests that you were right over the event horizon. Light cannot speed up when it falls into a black hole; after all, it's already flying at the speed of light. So the energy increases and the frequency rises toward the ultraviolet level."

"Doctor, can you speak more plainly? I can only follow half of what you're saying." The general sounded annoyed. "In particular, can you please tell me why only an hour-and-half have passed for him, and nearly twelve for us?"

"Because of the time dilation. When the gravitational force is that high, clocks, and time, move at a different speed. If he had been even closer to the event horizon, a minute in the black hole could have been a thousand years on Earth. I wish I could have seen that." The physicist whispered the last sentence, but the general was no longer listening. He turned back to Russell.

"I'm glad you returned safely, Harris. You should go and rest."

Russell walked toward Ellen, who had just come into the cave. She ran over to him and hugged him tightly.

"I thought I'd lost you," she whispered.

"I thought the same for a while. But I found my way back."

Ellen kissed him passionately on the mouth and Russell kissed her back.

Morrow, on the other hand, just shook his head and marched off to report the news. One by one, Russell's comrades hurried into the cave and inundated him with questions. Colonel Holbrook shooed them away and led Russell into the container where he helped him out of his space suit. He had to tell the colonel about his adventure again down to the last detail.

"Damn, Russell. You just wrote history. The first astronaut to visit a black hole. Even in my wildest dreams I've only got as far as circling the moon!"

"I'm not an astronaut, Christian."

"Oh yes you are. You're one of us now."

He spent the rest of the night with Ellen. Albert, who was due to start on the next mission in a few hours, stayed in the cave. Gilbert kept him company and analyzed Russell's data on his computer.

15. Albert

A few hours later, they met up again in the sphere to wish Albert a safe trip. The former pilot seemed calm and relaxed—perhaps because of the many dangerous flying missions that he'd completed in his lifetime.

"If you die, you die. I always got into the cockpit with that attitude. I'm old and have had enough opportunities to die. So what I'm about to do now doesn't bother me. The only difference is that I'm flying a bit further afield." With these words he turned around, climbed the steps and disappeared into the inner sphere without once looking back.

After two minutes, Gilbert started the transport at the agreed time. A few seconds later, the connection was broken. Albert Bridgeman had cut it off. Now the waiting began again. Russell went over to Gilbert, who seemed tired and distracted.

"Hey, Doc. You okay?"

The physicist turned to look at Russell.

"Yes, I'm fine. Just a bit exhausted. I didn't sleep too well the last few nights."

"Then we've got something in common. So, have you been able to find anything out from the data you've gathered so far?"

"No, not yet."

"But you've got comprehensive data from three missions. Surely you must have been able to get something out of it?"

"Well, it's not that easy. We have the data from each of the environments, but the most important thing is to work out the position of the destinations. We've analyzed the night sky from Ellen's mission. That will help us. From Walker's mission we could only see the nebula, which probably won't help us much. And from your trip to the black hole we probably also can't gain any reliable position data due to the movement and the blueshift of the stars. So far we haven't been able to find any information about the makers of the transporter."

"And what do you intend to do next?"

"I think we need to complete the first series of missions and then evaluate the data in peace. During the break, our astronauts will visit those destinations that have proven to be safe, and carry out further research. Let's wait and see."

Russell hoped that something would happen over the next few days. He didn't want to get back into the transporter. Or watch Ellen get back in. He also didn't believe that the five of them who remained would all survive their missions. At least Albert had good chances now, statistically.

Almost exactly an hour later, the former pilot returned. He climbed calmly out of the sphere, came down the steps and gave Gilbert his scanner. Russell hurried over to him.

"Well? Tell us what happened!"

"I took some good pictures of the stars. They better be of some use to those eggheads."

"Where were you?"

"On some planet. The gravity was a little lower than on Earth. I went down the rope into the outer sphere and had a look outside."

"And? Was there an atmosphere?"

"Nothing worth mentioning. Just traces of atomic hydrogen and oxygen. A little more than on the moon. When I went outside, the first thing I did was fall over. The ground was a giant sheet of ice that stretched from horizon to horizon. It was darn cold. Barely fifty Kelvin. The sun of the system was yellow like ours, but much further away—hardly more than a bright star. It certainly didn't give off any warmth. I took photos of the entire sky and left the monitoring devices there. Then I came back. Right, and now I'm hungry. What's for lunch?"

Albert trudged over to the container where Holbrook was already waiting at the entrance.

Russell shook his head.

Nothing fazed that guy!

The rest of the day passed relatively uneventfully. At supper, Russell sat beside Michael Bridges, who was next up for the transporter. He tried to get into a conversation with him, but Bridges seemed very distant. He thought no more of it and talked to Albert, who was sitting opposite him.

16. Bridges

During the night, Russell was suddenly woken up by the sound of alarm sirens. He jolted upright and looked at his watch. It was just before five a.m. Hurriedly he pulled on his jacket and ran outside. A truck full of soldiers had just arrived, and General Morrow was driving a Jeep past the guard post and into the compound.

"General. What happened?"

"Bridges knocked out one of the guards and escaped through the fence!"

"What are you going to do?"

"I've requested for a helicopter with thermal imaging equipment, which should be here any minute now. We'll find him. It's only a matter of minutes. Tell Rogers that he will take over the mission today."

"What will you do with Bridges?"

"He'll be taken to the military police base to be court-martialed and shot."

"Let me fly with you and talk to Bridges. He's scared. Give him a chance."

"Bridges has made his decision."

"General. Let me talk to him and I guarantee you that he will do his mission tomorrow. We haven't found out anything up to now. You can't afford to lose one of the volunteers."

Morrow considered. Russell knew that he'd hit the bulls-eye.

"Okay, come with me."

An old Bell UH-1D landed in front of the fence. Russell recognized the thermal imaging camera on the underside.

He and the general ran over to the helicopter and

sat down in the rear cabin. Two soldiers with sniper rifles were already sitting inside. The pilot took off and flew in a southerly direction. Morrow put on headphones with an integrated microphone and gave instructions.

"He'll try to get to the next road. Fly south. I don't know exactly when he escaped, but he can't have gone further than twenty miles. It's fifty miles to the next interstate, so we're sure to find him. Go to three-thousand feet and scan the whole area."

The pilot flew in big S-curves toward the road. After half an hour he reported back.

"I've got a signal. Switch on your screen."

Morrow activated a screen above one of the seats. At first, Russell could only see a blue fuzz. Then he was able to make out the red outline of a running man. Outside, dawn was already breaking and from the side window he could see Bridges, who was running toward the distant horizon.

"Put me on loudspeaker," said the general, before speaking to the runaway. "Bridges! Stop, or you will be shot immediately! We have snipers on board."

One of the soldiers who was secured by a harness, leant out of the helicopter and propped himself on one of the skids. He took his heavy gun and aimed.

"Ready, General."

Russell waved at the pilot to put him on loudspeaker too. "Bridges. Russell here. Stop—it's over. General Morrow is serious. Don't move, or you're a dead man."

Bridges slowed down and came to a halt. Angrily he shouted up at the helicopter, waving his fists.

"Leave me in peace. Fuck off!"

The helicopter landed about three-hundred feet away from him. Russell stepped out and walked calmly over to his comrade.

"There's no point—you must realize that. It's impossible to escape from here."

"I'm not getting into that fucking sphere!"

"Then they'll shoot you, man!"

"Then let them. Here and now. But I'm not climbing into that fucking thing! You saw what happened to O'Brien. I don't want to die like that!"

"At least that way you have a chance! Look. I survived. Ellen survived. Albert's alive."

"But I don't want to!"

"Nor did I. You were in the army. Each mission could have been your last."

"That was different!"

"Was it really? If you're so frightened, get Cummings to prescribe you a sedative before you get into the transporter. But if you refuse, the general will have you shot. He was about to order the snipers to shoot—I was only just able to stop him."

"How nice of you," said Bridges sarcastically.

"Jesus, use your chance! It's a mission! The chances of survival are now more than fifty-fifty."

"We have ten missions, Russell. Ten!"

"I'm convinced that Gilbert will find out how that thing works soon."

"Well I'm afraid I don't share your optimism!"

"Then at least share my realism, which says that you'll be shot if you don't come back!"

After some more back and forth, Bridges gave in. The general handcuffed him and two soldiers dragged him back to the helicopter. Soon they were back at the compound. Bridges was taken to his room and locked inside.

When Russell arrived in the cave with Morrow, Jim Rogers had just ended his mission. He had visited a planet with a breathable atmosphere and described his experiences.

"I'm telling you, I could have taken off my helmet. The pressure and the composition of the atmosphere were almost the same as on Earth. The sky was bright blue. There were a few little clouds on the horizon. It was a little chilly at minus four degrees Fahrenheit, but even that wouldn't have been a problem."

"Was there any sign of life? Animals or plants?" asked Gilbert.

"No, nothing. Just bare rock. Fairly high mountains on the horizon. Looked like the Himalayas."

"Perhaps you were in the Himalayas?"

"From there you wouldn't see two moons!"

"Oh."

"One moon was small, like ours, but had a brownish color. The other one was bigger. Probably also closer. It had a reddish color and migrated to the right across the sky. It looked like Mars. I took lots of photos."

"Our astronauts will go and check it out in more detail in the coming days," said Morrow. "Good job, Mr. Rogers."

Jim turned to Russell. "Did you find Bridges?"

"Yes, he's in his room. Tomorrow he'll be transported to the destination that was originally assigned to you."

Jim shrugged and went with Holbrook to the container.

The following morning, Morrow and Dr. Cummings went to collect the day's candidate from his room. Russell stood in the hallway and looked through the open door into Bridges' room. He sat on a chair trembling with wide-open eyes. The general was talking insistently to him. Then Bridges nodded and Dr. Cummings gave him an injection. Russell presumed it was a sedative. Almost immediately, Bridges stopped trembling. A few minutes later the three men left the room and went outside where the truck was waiting.

The others followed half an hour later. Together they marched on foot to the tunnel. Russell and Ellen fell behind a little. Ellen grabbed his hand.

"What's up? You seem so distracted," he said.

"I don't like the way they're treating Bridges. He was scared and his whole body was trembling. He was O'Brien's friend and he was really shaken by what happened to him. Now he's being taken to the transporter drugged up like an animal going to slaughter."

"What would you have done instead?"

"Probably nothing. In the end we all more or less volunteered."

"Yes, as far as a person condemned to death can 'volunteer', when he's offered a last chance," said Ellen cynically.

"I wonder if what's going on here is just."

Ellen burst out laughing. "Just? How do you define just? Is the death penalty just? Is what happened to my husband just? Or what you did to that drunkard who killed your family? Bridges made the same decision as we did when he volunteered for the project. He has the same chances of survival as we do, so wouldn't you say it's fair that he gets into the sphere like we did? You yourself stopped the general from shooting him and gave him another chance."

"I know. I totally agree with you. But I still think it's fucked up."

"In the past I volunteered to sit on a rocket. You volunteered for combat missions, in the knowledge that you might not come back alive. And that was when you still had a family."

"Yeah, you're right. And we got into the sphere voluntarily and didn't make a spectacle of ourselves. But when I saw Bridges this morning, I realized how fucked up this whole system is."

"Was it ever not? We all try to make the best of our lives. Whether it's President Bigby, who swung the election in his favor by promising to toughen the death penalty, or Bridges, who murdered people with O'Brien to get rich. Aren't they just as fucked up as Morrow and Gilbert, who are sending convicts to their probable deaths in the transporter, just in the hope of making some discovery? I don't want to think about it too much, it's just one big headache. So let's end this conversation, okay? At least for today."

Russell said nothing, but continued to mull it over.

When Bridges entered the outer sphere in his space suit, he stumbled perilously. Babbling to himself, he staggered up the steps to the transporter with a stupid grin on his face. Russell went over to Dr. Cummings.

"What on earth did you give him, Doctor?"

"A saline solution."

Russell looked at him wide-eyed. "Saline solution? Do you mean you gave him a placebo?"

Cummings nodded.

"So why is he babbling like he's drunk a bar dry?"

"The power of self-delusion, Harris."

Russell shook his head and went back to Ellen.

Gilbert started the transport and began the countdown. After a minute, Bridges still hadn't broken the connection so the physicist transported him back. Russell began walking up the steps. He assumed that Bridges simply hadn't been able to do anything at all, and expected to find him cowering in the sphere.

"Wait, Harris," voices came from behind him. Gilbert, Cummings, and the general caught up with him.

Russell opened the sphere.

"What the ...?"

In the transporter, it looked as if someone had sprayed the walls and ceiling with thick tomato juice. Red drops hung from long gloopy threads and dripped down in front of Russell. And from the arch of the sphere little scraps of flesh fell to the ground. Twisted pieces of equipment lay scattered around the sphere. The stench was unbearable. Russell's stomach lurched.

"Is that Bridges?" he asked. "Holy shit, it looks as if he's been through a grinder."

Cummings bent down and rubbed a drop of the red stuff between his thumb and forefinger. "It's blood. Without a doubt."

"Any idea what happened, Dr. Gilbert?" asked the general.

"Yes."

"Why doesn't that surprise me," murmured Russell.

"I think the man landed in an atmosphere with a very high pressure. Perhaps hundreds or thousands of bar. The pressure compressed him into a little ball. When the return transport started, the sudden change back to normal air pressure caused the mass to quickly expand. Bridges literally exploded."

The voice of the physicist sounded as if he were analyzing an interesting physical problem in a laboratory.

General Morrow turned around without another word and went down the steps. Behind him stood Jim Rogers, who now looked into the sphere.

"I guess I need to thank Bridges!"

"What do you mean?" asked Russell.

"If I hadn't jumped in for him yesterday, it would have been me who was transported to that juice extractor."

Following this incident, everyone gathered in Russell's room. They sat around the table, each clutching a drink of their choice. The atmosphere was somber.

"I've never chickened out of a mission," explained Russell. "I never had a problem with doing my duty. And I wasn't very understanding of soldiers who did wimp out. But what happened to Bridges really got to me."

He took another gulp of his beer. He had been glad when Jim and Albert had turned up at his door with a six-pack. He had been lost in dark thoughts all day. Now he wanted to know what his friends thought of it all.

"You think it's immoral to use condemned men for something like this?" asked Albert.

"I don't know," he replied. "Yesterday I would have said no. But since seeing Bridges this morning, I'm no longer so sure."

"He volunteered. He could have remained in his cell on death row," said Albert.

"You can't really call it a decision. None of us would have stayed in our cells voluntarily. Nobody would have said no to this opportunity."

Albert took a swig from his whiskey bottle, screwed the cap back on and put it down next to him on the floor.

"We used to all have jobs in which we could have died," he reminded the others. "I had a buddy who took off on a test flight with an F-16. As he shot along the runway his turbine blew up six feet behind him. The wreckage of the turbine blades punctured his tank and ignited the kerosene. Nothing burns hotter than kerosene! They couldn't find a trace of him. No bones, no teeth, nothing. One moment he was still a pilot, looking forward to a few beers at the end of the day, the next moment he was nothing but thin air. With no warning. It takes two seconds to notice something is wrong and activate the ejector seat. Bill didn't even have those two seconds. And yet the next morning, I still got into my plane. It's not so different from what we're doing here."

"Well, the odds are a little worse here," retorted Jim.

"But what do you think in general?" asked Russell. "Do you think it's right that we're being sent off in the transporter as guinea pigs?"

"I dunno what's right or wrong. If you ask me,

everything in this country is going to the dogs anyway."

"Yeah, right," said Albert sarcastically. "As a whistleblower you live by your own moral code, anyway!"

Russell smiled. It was strange that the arch-conservative test pilot and the liberal Jim got on so well. Even their constant jibing didn't seem to harm their friendship.

"I love my country," insisted Jim. "I'm proud of my country. But that shit thing those assholes wanted to install in orbit went against everything I believed in. With RedEye you could have murdered anyone you wanted on Earth and it would have looked like a heart attack!"

"Yeah, you told us."

"It's just not right."

"I know a few dictators in the world where I would have been glad to pull the trigger personally," said Albert.

"But who has the right to decide to use a thing like that? Those decisions are made in a back room of the NSA. Without any legal authority. What happens when a president like Bigby turns out to be a tyrant and in control of that kind of system? Nobody has the courage to revolt. Imagine if Hitler had had an instrument like that at his disposal. Imagine what the world would look like today."

"You can't compare the United States to Nazi Germany!"

"No, of course not. But many of the things going on in our country just aren't right. Especially since Bigby was elected. Take you and Russell: before Bigby, you would have got ten to twenty years at most for manslaughter. I would have done my ten years and would have got back out. Ellen wouldn't even have been convicted. Does it seem right to you? Has our country become a fairer place since the law was amended? Everyone has their own idea of morality and their own definition of justice. And I don't think it's right when a government starts to decide who should live and who should die. And it isn't even the government that decides, but the intelligence agency. It's all screwed up, and that's why I leaked the information to the public. I knew what could happen to me, and now I have to pay the price. Do I think it's right that I was almost turned into tomato juice today? No. But I shouldn't complain. If I don't abide by the system then I have to live with the consequences. And the same goes for Bridges."

Russell was impressed by Jim's self-conviction. He really seemed to have thought a lot about the meaning of morality. But then I guess you would have to if you were willing to put your life on the line for what you believed in. Or maybe he just had a screw loose.

17. Hilmers

The next man to climb into the transporter was Vance Hilmers. The striking face and bald head of the forty-four-year-old disappeared into the sphere without a word. As he entered the sphere with Holbrook he had already closed his visor, so Russell couldn't see the expression on the murderer's face. After Hilmers had been teleported, the connection was quickly broken off.

An hour later he returned safe and sound. He had been on a cold, gray planet. The gravitational pull was about the same as on earth, but there had been no atmosphere. He had had a good view of the stars and had been able to take some usable photos of the sky.

After his return, Gilbert took the monitoring device with a smile and disappeared into his laboratory container. Hilmers didn't have much to say about this trip. He fished a bottle of vodka out of the bag he had taken with him and drank half of it in big, thirsty gulps. He was already rat-arsed before he was able to take off his suit. Russell helped Holbrook take the man to his room. He wasn't seen for the rest of the day.

18. Rushworth

The following Monday it was John Rushworth's turn. He looked in bad shape when he arrived at the sphere. He had dark rings under his eyes and his expression was glazed. Russell could see right away that he was frightened. The former soldier went up the steps to the transporter with trembling legs, looked back once more with a hunted look on his face, closed his visor and disappeared into the transporter. After a short countdown, Gilbert started the transport. Russell stood beside him.

"Doc, you look tired."

"I spent the whole night evaluating Hilmers' data."

"And?"

"They're the best photos of the stars we've had so far. With data like that, we must be able to work out the planet's position."

"Rushworth seems to be in difficulty. There's still a connection and it's been forty seconds."

"Yes, I'll prepare the return transport. Ten seconds."

Damn, damn.

"Return transport in progress," said Gilbert in an emotionless voice.

We're just not making any progress, thought Russell with pursed lips. *Now we might even be one man down.*

Together with Gilbert and Dr. Cummings he hurried up the steps and opened the sphere. There was a burnt smell. Cautiously, and with a queasy feeling in his stomach, Russell peered through the opening.

All that was left of Rushworth were some

charred remains scattered across the floor. And where the monitoring devices had been standing a minute earlier there were now puddles of strange substances.

With an inquisitive look on his face, the physicist went over to one of the steaming spots and held his hand over it.

"Hot," he muttered. "That's melted metal from one of our instruments; this is where the spotlight was. Obviously Rushworth came out in an atmosphere with a temperature of over six-thousand degrees Fahrenheit. Even the tungsten wires of the light bulbs have melted away."

The doctor stooped over the charred remains of the man and poked them with a ballpoint pen. They were still steaming and giving off heat.

"It must have happened very quickly," the doctor said. "He didn't feel a thing."

Russell asked himself which was worse: to be aware that you were about to die, if only for a moment, or to stop existing from one moment to the next.

19. Williams

The evening before the last transport, there was a knock at Russell's door. It was George Williams, the last of the group to go on a mission. Russell was surprised to see him, since up to now Williams had never showed any inclination to talk to him. Russell asked him in, and the two men sat down.

"I want to ask you a favor, Harris," he said.

Russell offered him a can of beer, but his visitor declined.

"Thanks, I don't drink out of principle." Instead he took a letter out of his jacket pocket and handed it to Russell. Russell took it and held it uncertainly. There was a woman's name on the back of the envelope.

"What is it?"

"I want to ask you to get this letter to my wife if I die tomorrow. I know that any form of communication is strictly forbidden, but I know you get on well with the physicist. Ask him to keep the letter until the grass has grown over this project. Then he should send it to my wife. There's nothing in the letter about the project, but I want to have the chance to tell her how much she means to me and how grateful I am to her."

Russell nodded understandingly. "I'll try. But one question: Why don't you ask Jim? He's built up some good contacts here, and you guys were friends, weren't you?"

"Yes, we were … once."

"What happened? Didn't you work together to leak those documents about the military satellite?"

Williams eyes narrowed to slits and a vein bulged on

his forehead. "Together? Don't make me laugh. He tried to convince me, and I always refused. I have a family and I wanted to be with them. I knew what would happen if I joined him. I didn't agree with that damn satellite project, but I'm not a martyr like James. I told him if he wants to act the hero, he has to go it alone. But he needed my access codes to get to the data. And that motherfucker stole them from me."

Russell didn't respond, but looked at his enraged comrade in silence.

"Because he used my code I was accused of being his co-conspirator. Since that day I've only seen my wife once. She accused me of not only betraying our country but also our family. Her attorney was with her, and kept applying the pressure until I signed the divorce papers." He swallowed. A single tear ran down his cheek. "The fact is, I still love her and never wanted to betray our family. In jail I could have spoken to her one more time before my execution. Here that isn't possible."

"Thanks for being so open. But don't give up hope."

"I won't. But my chances aren't looking great." Williams got up and went to the door. There he turned around again and looked Russell straight in the eye. "Thank you."

Then he was gone. Russell sat down on his bed and finished his beer, lost in thought.

Nothing is as it seems.

The following morning they gathered again in the sphere. Of the group of ten, there were only six remaining after nine missions. Russell Harris, Ellen Slayton, Albert Bridgeman, Jim Rogers, and Vance

Hilmers stood in the outer sphere to wish George Williams a safe trip. Jim stood slightly apart, and Russell could see in his face that he was preoccupied. When William entered the sphere accompanied by Holbrook, Jim turned away. Williams nodded to Russell and got ready to go up the steps.

"George." Jim Rogers hurried over to his old friend, who stopped at the foot of the steps and turned around, not even looking surprised. The two men talked for a few minutes, but they were too far away for Russell to catch more than a few words. In the end it was Williams who took off the glove of his space suit and grasped the fingers of his former friend. The two men looked at each other for a few seconds. Then Williams nodded and climbed the steps. On his way up he pulled his glove back on and pulled down his visor. He disappeared into the transporter and closed the opening behind him.

Gilbert started the countdown. The physicist's face had changed in the last few days. It had become harder. He had lost his playful curiosity of just a week ago and now exuded only cool professionalism. Sending four men to their deaths at the touch of a button was bound to take its toll. And now Gilbert pressed on the button again and started Williams' transport. The return transport was activated just a few moments later.

Oh, he must have come out somewhere terrible.

Russell and the others waited for their colleague to open the sphere and re-emerge, but nothing happened.

In the end it was Jim Rogers who slowly climbed the steps and opened the sphere. Russell, Gilbert and Cummings followed him.

"George!" Jim cried in alarm.

Williams lay on the floor. His space suit was steaming as if he had been laid in boiling water. Jim rushed over to him and wanted to take off his helmet, but then he cried out in pain.

"What is it?" asked Gilbert. "Is he hot?"

"No, ice-cold," gasped Jim with panic in his voice. "There, can you see? When I pulled my hand away, bits of skin stayed stuck to his suit."

"Get away from there." Dr. Cummings pushed his way to his side and knelt over Williams. He took out a pair of gloves from his bag and pushed open the visor.

Williams' face was clearly recognizable. He looked as if he had been in cold storage for months. His face was covered in ice-crystals and a vapor rose from his helmet. Gilbert got some tools and together they prized the helmet off. In the process a frozen ear fell off and hit the ground with a tinkling sound.

Cummings shook his head. "There's nothing we can do. The man is dead."

"How can that be?" Russell also shook his head. "Even if he came out in an icy atmosphere, the insulation of the suit should have protected him. He can't have been turned into a block of ice in the space of a few seconds. What happened?"

"I can answer that question," said Gilbert, who was looking at Williams' equipment and reading the last values on the scanner before it, too, gave up the ghost. "He was in liquid nitrogen. The temperature was around minus three-hundred degrees Fahrenheit. The space suit protected him for a few seconds, but the protective layers couldn't withstand the ice-cold liquid for long and became brittle. When Williams moved, the seams ripped and the nitrogen got into the space suit. I'm surprised he was even able to start the return transport. But perhaps it was precisely that movement which caused his suit to rip. The inside of the suit is still full of the stuff."

Russell turned on his heel.

And then there were five.

20. Limbo

Late in the evening a meeting was called. The atmosphere was subdued. Ellen had dark rings under her eyes and Jim's face was puffy, as if he had been crying all day—which was possibly the case. Russell had never felt so drained. General Morrow stood in front of the five remaining candidates and began to speak.

"The first ten transports have been completed. We are suspending the missions for fourteen days. In this time, Dr. Gilbert will analyze the data we have collected so far, and Holbrook and our astronauts will visit those destinations which, thanks to your help, we know are safe. You can now rest for two days, then Sergeant Niven will start your exercise regime again. But I can reassure you that that it won't be as tough as two weeks ago. At the end of the fourteen days we will discuss the findings, and based on the results we will decide whether and when further transports will take place." He paused before adding: "I must admit that I expected the survival rate to be higher. But I hope that the death of your fallen comrades was not in vain. Do you have any questions?"

Jim looked up. "How is Walker?"

"Robert Walker is lying in the military hospital and is being cared for. However, his condition is worsening. He is only sporadically conscious. We have brought in specialists from Los Alamos who are familiar with radiation poisoning, but the dosage was so high that there is no cure. The doctors assume that he will die within the next three days."

Russell nodded. It's what he had expected.

Morrow turned around and left the room.

"Jesus! What do we do now?" hissed Jim. There was nothing left of his humor and his laid-back manner. Something inside him had broken when he had discovered his friend dead in the transporter.

"What do you think?" said Russell. "We wait and see what Gilbert and his team find out."

"What if they don't find anything?" asked Jim. "Do you think they'll stick us back in the transporter?"

"I have no idea. I reckon the general will fight our corner."

Albert stood up and went to the window. "Well, I reckon they'll find out something useful. I don't want to believe that five of us died for nothing."

"And what if that's the case?" whispered Jim. "Maybe we should start thinking about whether there's any chance of escape before push comes to shove."

"Forget it," warned Albert. "Morrow will be expecting that. After Bridges' attempt he'll have taken every precaution."

"I'm starting to understand O'Brien when he said that he didn't want to set foot in the transporter ever again ..."

"Please, Jim, don't get worked up. Let's wait and see what Gilbert finds out."

"I'm not getting worked up. I'm just saying we should have a plan if worst comes to the worst." His voice was becoming louder with every word he spoke.

"I don't want to carry on with this conversation," Albert said curtly, and left the room.

Jim followed him, but continued talking to him outside. Vance Hilmers shrugged and also left. Russell and Ellen were left alone.

He went over to her. She hadn't said a word the whole time. He sat down beside her in silence and tried to take her hand, but she pulled it away.

"Is everything okay?"

She nodded. "Yes, I'm just tired. So very tired. The last few days were such a white-knuckle ride, I don't know anymore what to think. Four of us are dead. Another will be dead in a few days, and we shouldn't rule out that it will continue like that until we're all dead."

Her voice was toneless, he couldn't detect even a tinge of emotion. Her eyes were also expressionless. She had retreated into herself.

"Do you agree with Jim that we should be searching for alternatives?"

She shrugged. "I only know that I don't want to get back into that damn sphere. I don't want to go through that again, and I don't want to have to watch anyone else getting in. But I also think that we need to wait and see if Gilbert can find anything out, or if the general can do anything to help us."

She stood up.

"Would you like me to come to your room?" he asked.

She smiled at him, but it was a forced smile. "No, Russell. Not tonight. I want to be alone. Can you understand that?"

"Of course."

When he fell into bed that evening he felt old and exhausted. He drifted into a fitful sleep and when he awoke the next day he didn't have the feeling of being rested.

After breakfast, Dr. Cummings appeared and told the group that Robert Walker had died during the night as a result of his radiation poisoning. The mood dropped to an all-time low. There was nothing to do that day and everyone brooded on their own.

The next few days dragged by. Sergeant Niven began to torment the group with exercises, races, and marches.

Russell noticed that Ellen was retreating from him. He put it down to the pressure and uncertainty and left her in peace. Jim, for his part, was very testy. It was hardly possible to say a word to him without him getting angry. Even Albert had changed. He had always been a little calmer and more levelheaded than the rest, but these days he hardly spoke at all, and like Ellen, he withdrew into himself.

On the other hand, Russell was surprised that his relationship with Vance Hilmers was improving. He presumed the guy was a follower type, who needed someone to look up to. Once, this had been O'Brien, which had made him unbearable, but now the former burglar had turned his attention to Russell and become more agreeable. During a march through the scorching sun they chatted.

"I've always hated these marches," said Hilmers. "I liked being in the army, but I despised the constant marching."

"Were you in Afghanistan?"

"No, I was in a support unit in Iraq. I was a truck-driver—drove stuff back and forth across the Euphrates and Tigris."

"Support unit? You never took part in combat missions?"

Hilmers laughed out loud. "I didn't need to go looking for them. Twice my truck was blown up beneath me. Fucking attacks. Once I was transporting half a ton of ammunition. It's a miracle I'm still alive. And we'd barely escaped from the burning wreckage, when the Hajis started to fire at us. I had a few narrow escapes."

"How did you end up in jail?"

"After my term of service, I had nothing to do. So I hung around and drank and smoked pot. A friend thought we should get ourselves some money and break into a few houses. We were just trying to crack a safe in some fancy villa when the owner came back. We tried to get out, but he started screaming to wake the whole neighborhood. At that moment, I lost my nerve and shot him. Then we got out." He laughed again. "We were such amateurs. Neither Frank nor I noticed that there was a surveillance system in the house. Less than an hour later, a task force stormed my apartment. Now I'm getting what I deserve. It's as simple as that."

"How much money did you take from the safe?"

Hilmers laughed again. "Nothing. It was empty."

They spent the rest of their free time walking together in the heat until the sun went down and they returned to the base.

A few days later Russell saw Dr. Gilbert hurrying across the compound with a pile of papers. He ran after him.

"Hey Doc. Wait a minute."

"Oh, hi Russell. I don't have much time, I'm on my way to a phone conference."

"Just quickly, Doc. How's it looking? Have you found anything out yet?"

The physicist shook his head. "It's too early.

We've evaluated the photos of the stars and transferred them to the computer. To work out the position of the destinations in the galaxy we've set up a Monte-Carlo simulation on a mainframe computer. It'll take a few days until we have the results. And now please excuse me. I'll let you know as soon as I find anything out."

"Thanks."

The physicist disappeared into a building and Russell returned to his room, his mind in overdrive.

21. The Bomb

A few days later, Russell drove with Colonel Holbrook down into the cave to check the space suits with him. As they worked, the astronaut told him about his transport the day before. He had visited Ellen's planet.

"It was really a phenomenal sight. When you step out of the transporter, you're standing in this red landscape—it reminded me of the pictures I've seen of Mars. And then there's this gigantic Saturn-like planet in the sky. It's quite something, Russell!"

"What did you do there?"

"We set up cameras that will take photographs of the sky in higher resolution. And by the way, Gilbert thinks he has worked out the position of the planets in the galaxy."

"Really?"

"Yes. It seems we are slowly making progress."

It was the first bit of good news in a long time. But would it get them any closer to working out how the transporter worked?

Russell cleaned the valves of the space suit with a damp cloth, oiled them carefully and reinserted them. To finish, they carried out an impermeability test by subjecting the suits to high pressure.

On the way back through the cave, he saw Dr. Gilbert through the window of his container. He decided to pay the physicist a visit and knocked at the door of his office.

"I just saw you with Colonel Holbrook. Come in. I've got something interesting to show you."

The physicist was sitting in front of his computer. On the screen was a diagram of the Milky

Way. Russell pulled up a stool next to him.

Gilbert tapped on the screen with a pen. "We're here. This is our solar system. And here, on the edge of the center of the Milky Way is the black hole that you visited."

"You were really able to work out the position?"

"Yes, more or less. It's around thirty-thousand light years away."

"Unbelievable!"

"We scanned in static images from your high-resolution helmet camera and corrected the blueshift and movement of the stars on the computer. Here. There are lots of stars. Nowhere are the suns so densely packed together as in the center of the Milky Way." He pointed at a spot on the screen. "This is the center. The perspective is similar to how it looks from Earth, so you must have come out somewhere around here. Precise to the nearest thousandth light year, I would say."

"And how does that help us?"

"We've also been able to work out the positions of Ellen's and Albert's planets. With the help of the pulsars and the neighboring galaxies we could work out the positions to the nearest few dozen light years. We've had cryptologists and cosmologists trying to discover a connection between the positions and the codes. Here, look at this."

The physicist rummaged around in a pile of papers and photos.

Russell felt uneasy. It was all well and good that they'd worked out the positions of the planets, but even if you could work out a connection to the destination code, it wouldn't help them know whether a destination was dangerous or not.

The physicist riffled through another pile of paper, muttering to himself. Meanwhile Russell looked around. The container laboratory was very untidy. There was equipment lying around everywhere and control panels on the walls. Cables were routed through the walls, disappeared into the floor, or led to the sphere. He noticed a small control panel in the corner.

I know that thing. That's a detonating device for …

"Hey Doc, have a you got an atomic bomb hidden away here?"

The physicist turned around and followed Russell's gaze. He put his papers down on the table and nodded.

"Yes, we have. The general insisted on it."

"And where is the bomb?"

"Underneath the cave in another hollow. It's a hydrogen bomb. A W88 warhead with an energy equivalent of half a megaton."

"What the hell for?"

"The general is afraid that an army of invaders might come marching out of that thing. Total nonsense if you ask me. But he insisted on it." The physicist showed him a chain that he wore around his neck with a key hanging from the end of it. "The general also has one. When both keys have been inserted, you have thirty minutes to leave the cave. Once it's activated, it can no longer be defused. The explosive agent is buried directly beneath the sphere. Typical military paranoia in my opinion." He tucked the key away and carried on looking through his papers.

Russell shook his head. But he agreed with General Morrow; the man considered all eventualities—and once that had saved his life.

Now the physicist placed a photo on the table. "You see, this is a picture of the radioactive nebula, which was Walker's undoing. Here, too, we were able to filter out the stars on the computer and work out the position. I'll be excited to see what connections our specialists can make to the destination code."

Russell was no longer listening. He couldn't stop thinking about the nuclear weapon buried under the sphere and wondered in what situation the general would detonate the bomb.

22. Despair

The following days passed by monotonously. Sergeant Niven bullied the group through the hot desert sand without breaks. There was no more news about the project. Finally, on the fourteenth day, something happened. But it wasn't anything that raised Russell's hopes. He noticed that security was increasing. There were more soldiers walking around the compound.

That evening, General Morrow called a meeting. Russell was on edge; he noticed that guards had been stationed in front of the meeting room and at the entrance to the accommodation block.

Morrow hovered in the background while Dr. Gilbert began to talk. His didn't look very happy.

"As you know, we were able to work out the position of four of the destinations. Our astronauts have visited each of the destinations again in order to carry out further measurements and to search for clues as to who built the transporter." The physicist looked at the floor. "Unfortunately we have not been able to find any evidence on this front. I also regret to have to inform you that our cryptologists cannot find any correlations between the position of the destinations and the respective symbol codes. I'm sorry. We need more information."

Russell could feel the blood draining from his face. He knew what was coming next. The general stepped forward.

"I've spoken with my superiors at the Pentagon, but the decision was ultimately made by President Bigby. The transports will continue tomorrow."

The group became agitated. Jim Rogers

whispered something to Albert.

The general coughed. "I did all I could to reduce the number of missions, but the President insists on sticking to the original plan of ten missions per person."

"That means we will all die," said Ellen drily.

Albert nodded bitterly. "We had five deaths in ten missions. Two or three of us will survive the next round. In the end there will only be one person left and he will probably die on the mission after that."

"No," said the general. "The President has agreed to pardon the final survivor and to reduce his sentence to life imprisonment."

Jim laughed out loud. "Well, we've really got something to look foreword to then!" He leaned over to Russell and whispered quietly: "Let's get out of here. It's our only chance."

The general continued speaking.

"I'm sorry that I wasn't able to achieve more. I would have reached a different decision, but it wasn't in my hands. But I do want to make one thing clear." He paused and looked each of them in the eye. "I am assuming that you are considering trying to escape. I will do everything in my power to prevent this. We have increased the number of guards, and you may only leave the building with somebody accompanying you."

"You really want to send us to the slaughter?" asked Jim.

"As I already said, it is out of my hands. The transports will continue tomorrow. The order in which you carry them out will stay the same. So Ms. Slayton will make a start tomorrow. And as I said already: I'm sorry."

He turned around and left the room. Gilbert followed him.

Russell sat as if turned to stone on his chair. The others were also stunned. He had reckoned with everything, but still couldn't believe they were now being sent blindly to their deaths … He simply didn't want to believe it. And to top it off, escaping was now definitely off the cards.

"We should have got out while we still had a chance," grumbled Jim.

"We wouldn't have got far. You saw how quickly they got Bridges!" Albert reminded him.

"We would have just had to do it a bit more intelligently. But now the horse has bolted. It's over. We're done for." He left the room, with Albert and Hilmers shuffling behind him.

Russell and Ellen were last to leave the meeting room. They were accompanied to their accommodation wing by guards who locked the connecting door behind them.

Imprisoned again. Back on death row.

Ellen hadn't said anything but Russell knew that she didn't want to be alone that night. For the first time in days they lay together in the same bed.

Ellen cried. Russell held her tightly in his arms. They didn't talk much. There was nothing more to say. He couldn't bear the idea of watching Ellen climb into the transporter tomorrow. He briefly considered not going down to the cave at all, but quickly abandoned the idea. He couldn't do that to her.

They lay beside each other in silence. The night passed without either of them once closing their eyes.

23. Revelation

Holbrook collected Ellen before dawn. She left without saying a word. Russell sat with Albert, Vance, and Jim in the little mess, where they ate their breakfast in silence. Suddenly he was overcome by a terrible thought.

Please let the others die in the sphere before me.

He despised himself for having this thought, but the others were probably thinking the same. They were competitors now. Each for his own. And the last one would survive.

A life in jail. What a future …

For the first time he really regretted agreeing to this project. It hadn't been an opportunity. It was a horror film.

After breakfast the truck drove them down to the cave. Once again they stood in the sphere and waited for a comrade to put her life on the line in this hellish machine. And on top of that he could feel a headache coming on again because that damn thing emitted some kind of waves.

Hang on. Headache?

Something nagged at him, but he couldn't put his finger on it.

In the background, General Morrow stood flanked by two guards with machine guns at their chests. Gilbert had programmed the new destination and was waiting. Engineer Blumberg was looking over at the guards with a stern expression.

Then Ellen entered the sphere in her space suit, accompanied by Holbrook. The astronaut looked at the general grimly. He looked like he was about to say something, but then didn't. His face clearly said what he thought about the continuation of the transports.

Ellen looked over at Russell. She tried to smile, but didn't succeed. He nodded at her encouragingly, although he had never felt quite so sick.

This is crazy. She's being sent off like an animal to slaughter.

Ellen climbed up the steps and disappeared into the transporter. After closing the sphere behind her, Gilbert began the countdown.

"One more minute."

Damn, damn.

Russell felt anger boiling up inside him. Anger toward Morrow, who couldn't stop this madness; anger toward Bigby, who had no problem sacrificing them all for his crazy experiment. He also felt angry with the unknown builders of this sphere and about this damn headache.

"Fifteen more seconds."

This damn headache. Why is it so bad again today?

"Ten more seconds."

The last time it was this bad was when …

"Five more seconds, four, three …" Gilbert's right hand approached the alien console.

A thought raced with incredible force through Russell's mind, followed by a jolt as if a nuclear bomb was being ignited.

"STOP!" He threw himself onto the physicist and ripped his hand from the control panel. "Don't activate it!"

Gilbert looked at him in bewilderment and Blumberg stood beside him open-mouthed.

Russell stormed up the steps, opened the sphere and ripped the surprised Ellen out of the sphere. "Get out of there at once!"

"Harris, for God's sake!" General Morrow had appeared beside him on the steps and was shouting at him. "Explain yourself immediately! Otherwise I will have you taken away!"

One of the guards grabbed Russell's arms and pulled him down the steps, but he looked unflinchingly at the physicist. "The headaches, Gilbert! Haven't you noticed?"

"What's with the headaches? I already told you they probably result from the high-frequency electromagnetic field of the sphere."

"Yes, but the headaches aren't always this strong. Don't you see? The last time it was this bad is when Williams died. And before that with Rushworth. And with Walker and O'Brien, too!"

"What are you saying?"

"When Ellen went into the transporter the last time I hardly had a headache; it was the same with Albert and Hilmers. That can't be a coincidence!"

"Well, I don't know …" began Gilbert and turned to Blumberg who looked back at him in bewilderment.

"Harris, if this is a trick in order to spare your girlfriend from going on her mission, then …"

"Set the destination code of Ellen's last mission!" Russell urged the physicist. "Go on, do it!"

Gilbert hesitated, then leafed through his notebook and changed the code on the control panel.

At first Russell didn't notice anything, but soon his pounding headache disappeared completely, until he only felt a light pressure on his temples.

Gilbert looked from him to the general. "I see what you mean. I can feel it, too. Oh Jesus." The physicist slapped himself on the forehead. "And nobody noticed it!"

The general shook his head in confusion. "Well, I don't notice any difference. What's going on?"

"I can feel it too," said the guard who was still holding Russell by the arm, quietly.

Morrow's looked baffled. "Are you trying to say that …?"

"… that the machine is communicating with us," Dr. Cummings finished the sentence. "Yes, and we were too stupid to notice it."

The general stood there, flabbergasted. Russell had never seen him so flustered. The others were also stunned. Ellen stood beside the steps, a look of shock on her face, Albert had his eyes closed, lost in thought, and Jim looked at Russell open-mouthed.

Gilbert had pulled himself together again and was back in his element. He couldn't stop babbling.

"Perhaps the constructors of this thing have been communicating with us through a sort of telepathy. Through electromagnetic waves. Yes, that must be it."

"What are you talking about?" said Morrow crossly.

"We're such idiots. Such idiots, for God's sake!" Gilbert looked as if he wanted to box his own ears.

"Speak plainly, man," said the general impatiently.

"The headaches come from the electromagnetic radiation."

"Yes, you said that already."

"By means of the electromagnetic radiation, the transporter is trying to communicate with us. Perhaps the constructers had a magnetic organ and communicated with each other via these electromagnetic waves. The same way we use sound waves to communicate. Do you understand, General? And we 'hear' this sphere through our headaches."

"And the strong headache today?"

"The sphere was trying to urgently warn us not to send Ellen to the programmed destination!" said Russell.

There was complete silence for a few seconds. Russell looked at the general and finally he could see comprehension spreading across his face.

"Dr. Gilbert, Dr. Cummings, and Colonel Holbrook," Morrow continued in a sober tone of voice. "Please follow me to the laboratory container. I wish to speak to you."

Together, the men disappeared into the makeshift room.

When they were gone, Ellen came over to Russell. She grasped his hand and whispered into his ear.

"Thank you."

An hour later, the door of the container opened and General Morrow hurried out. He stopped when he reached Russell.

"There will be no transports today. I need to discuss this with my superiors at the Pentagon. That was good work, Harris! But we need to check if your hypothesis is true." And with these words he hurried to the entrance of the tunnel.

That afternoon, Russell and Ellen were sitting in front of the accommodation block. The sun was already starting to set, and the wall threw long shadows that protected them from the scorching sun.

"Do you think the transporter was really trying to

warn us about a death trap with the headaches?" asked Ellen.

"It certainly seems that way."

"Then it also means that you saved my life today."

"It was pure self-interest!"

"No, I'm serious. Thank you."

"No worries."

"What do you think will happen now?"

"At some point we'll probably have to prove the assumption. That means we'll have to go on more transports. But only to destinations that don't cause any headaches. If nobody has died after a few missions, then I suppose it will prove my theory. Then we'll all live, finish our ten missions and be free!"

She smiled. "We can hope again. And this morning I thought it was all over."

"Me too. I could hardly bear to see you climbing into the transporter."

Ellen pulled her chair closer to his. "If we're allowed to hope again, then maybe we can plan our futures some time."

"Perhaps it could be a shared future?"

Her lips brushed softly against his. "I'd like that."

Dr. Gilbert ran past them. He was carrying a device with two long antennae.

"How's it going, Doc?"

"Hello Russell, I'm totally over the moon! That was really a wonderful surprise today!"

Russell shook his head incredulously.

A wonderful surprise? Ellen had escaped death by a whisker. What world are you living in? I should throw you in the transporter and press the button!

He pulled himself together.

"Yes, it really was a surprise," he said, trying to sound friendly. "But what have you got there?"

"A sensitive receiver for high-frequency radio waves. We want to analyze the radiation and see if we can discover a pattern in the waves. We are transferring the waves onto the computer and carrying out a Fourier analysis ..."

"Great, Doc. Have you heard anything from the general?"

"Oh, yes. The transports have been stopped for now, until we've got a better grasp of the situation. I think he wants to talk to you later on."

The physicist hurried to his car and drove off.

24. Test Mission

Two days later Russell was standing in his space suit next to Gilbert at the control pillar of the transporter. He had volunteered to carry out his mission before Ellen to prove that his theory was correct.

General Morrow stood beside them and spoke to the physicist. "What's the plan, Dr. Gilbert?"

"We've established that not everyone is equally sensitive to the EM radiation. Mr. Harris was of course the first person to notice the different strengths of the headaches. I am also sensitive to the variations, as is Dr. Cummings. Yesterday we set all the previous destinations and all three of us noticed a link between the extent of the pressure in our heads and the danger of the destinations."

"And what about your measurements? Have you been able to determine anything from these?"

"No, we haven't been able to glean anything from the measurements. The computer has only picked up high-frequency noise. Perhaps the sampling rate is too low. I've requested special equipment that ought to arrive in the next few days."

"And I've asked for an MRT, which should arrive tomorrow," added the doctor.

"An MRT?" asked the general.

"A magnetic resonance tomography machine. We want to measure the effect of the radiation on the brain. Perhaps we can find a way of communicating with the sphere."

The general looked at Russell doubtfully. "Wouldn't you rather wait for these results? I could arrange for the transports to be postponed. The reasons ought to be good enough to convince my superiors."

Russell shook his head. "We are absolutely convinced that we've found a connection. We really want to prove it."

"Okay. It's your decision, Harris."

"Great," said Gilbert and stared at the control panel. "We just set the destination code of this sphere. I only feel a slight pressure."

"Me too," said Russell.

"Same for me," confirmed the doctor.

Gilbert changed the code. "And this is the code for the destination that Ms. Slayton was due to visit."

Russell closed his eyes and concentrated. At first nothing happened. Then he felt a pounding sensation in the middle of his forehead.

"Clear headache," he replied. Gilbert and Cummings agreed.

Gilbert changed the code several times. "And this is the code for the star that we have selected for Mr. Harris' mission."

Russell felt the painful hammering subside—as if someone was slowly turning down the volume on a stereo system. After a while he only felt a light pressure in his temples.

"Yes, that's much better," he said.

Gilbert nodded. Cummings agreed.

Russell picked up his helmet from the ground. "Then let's find out."

He glanced around again and looked Ellen in the eyes. She was smiling but looked concerned.

What if I'm mistaken?

He climbed up the steps, entered the transporter and closed the opening.

One minute.

He was nervous, but wasn't filled with the fear of death like last time. He now had a similar feeling to the ones he'd had before combat missions in the past. He had a realistic chance.

Thirty seconds. But what if I made a mistake?

He switched on his scanner and activated the helmet camera.

Ten. Nine. Eight.

"Don't let me screw this up!" he said quietly to himself.

One. Zero.

He felt a slight jolt—as if he was standing in an elevator that was going down.

I'm alive. I was right.

Russell looked at the scanner. 0.75 g. An atmosphere with a pressure of 0.8 bar. Nitrogen 80 percent. Oxygen 15 percent. Carbon-dioxide 0.1 percent. No poisonous trace elements.

Damn it, I could take off my helmet here!

He cut off the connection and opened the opening to the outer sphere. It was empty, but he hadn't expected anything different.

He fastened the rope to the control panel of the transporter, went through the opening and let himself down slowly.

At least it's not another black hole. Let's see what it looks like outside.

He stood at the wall, hesitated a moment and then placed his hand on the outer wall. An opening appeared and he peered outside.

Wow. What a view!

He was looking at a landscape of low, gently rolling hills covered in a carpet of bright-green grass.

Up above, a red sun hovered close to the horizon in a pink-colored sky and gave off a pleasant warmth. The grass swayed gently in the breeze and little white clouds drifted slowly across the sky. All of the colors were almost surreally bright. It was a landscape out of a children's film; he almost expected big teddy bears with outstretched arms to come running down one of the hills.

He got out his camera and took video footage and lots of photos: of the landscape, the sky, and the sphere. Afterwards, he kneeled down to take a closer look at the grass. Carefully he brushed his fingers across the thin blades. They looked strange: on the one hand, thin and green like blades of grass on Earth, but on the other hand, utterly alien. He couldn't make out any kind of pattern or structure.

From a compartment on the scanner he took out a little container, which was meant for soil samples, and ripped out a few blades of grass.

Strange. They didn't have any roots. Only things that looked like suckers.

He pulled out a few more bunches of grass to look at the ground. Underneath the grass there wasn't any soil, like on Earth, but only bare rock.

Weird.

He put the vials with the samples in a bag of his space suit and continued looking around. It was the first planet on which they had found something living. In fact it was the first ever place apart from Earth to show signs of life. It dawned on him that he was the first person to discover alien life, and couldn't wipe the grin from his face.

Not bad for a former death-row inmate.

Despite his space suit he could feel a slight

breeze. It tempted him to simply open his helmet and breathe in the air of this strange planet.

Should I risk it?

He decided against it. At a leisurely pace he climbed up the nearest hill. After a few minutes he reached the top and looked around. He could see hills, and this strange grass blowing in the wind, as far as the eye could see. He took further measurements and series of photos, then returned to the transporter and back to Earth.

An amazed Gilbert took the samples and held the transparent vial up to the light.

"I may not be a biologist, but I have to look at that under the microscope." With these words he disappeared into his laboratory container.

General Morrow clapped Russell on the back. "It seems you were right, Harris."

His comrades surrounded him, patted him on the back and hugged him. For the first time in weeks there was a ray of hope in their faces.

25. Ellen's Second Mission

The next day it was Ellen's turn. She was nervous but confident. She stood next to Russell, Dr. Gilbert, and Dr. Cummings in her space suit. The physicist had set a destination code and now the three men concentrated on the pressure in their heads.

"The pressure isn't as strong as with the fatal destinations, but I'd rather set a different code," said Russell.

"Agreed," said Gilbert and changed the code.

Ellen looked attentively at the faces of the men and turned to the general who was standing behind her. "I have to admit, I don't notice any difference between the destinations. Not with any of them."

"It's the same for me, Ms. Slayton," whispered the general. "It really seems as if not all people are susceptible to this radiation."

"That code is better," said Russell. "Only a slight pressure in my head, very similar to my destination yesterday."

"Yes, I agree," said Cummings.

"Okay, then let's go with that destination," confirmed Gilbert and jotted something down in his notepad.

Ellen stroked Russell's back briefly before climbing up the steps. The physicist did the usual countdown and initiated the transport. Just a few seconds later the connection was cut off from Ellen's end.

"Now we have to wait again," murmured Dr. Cummings and went back to join the paramedics.

Russell stepped up to the physicist. "Could you make anything of the samples I brought you yesterday, Doc?"

"Yes," he replied. "They're very interesting. I may not be a biologist, but what I could see through the microscope was fascinating."

"I can imagine. It's a completely different grass from ours."

"Well, yes, it's not even really grass. To be honest it's not even a plant."

"You're not trying to tell me these things are animals?"

The physicist chuckled softly. "No, they aren't animals either. They're protozoa."

"Protozoa?"

"Yes, gigantic prokaryotes to be more precise— unicellular organisms without a nucleus. Under the microscope I could recognize something like DNA floating around in a kind of cytoplasm."

"That doesn't mean anything to me, Doc."

"It doesn't matter. I'm not a specialist either. I sent the sample to an exobiologist friend of mine at NASA. He'll be amazed." The physicist chuckled softly, then continued: "What's interesting is that these cells carry out photosynthesis as well as aerobic respiration. So they emit both oxygen and carbon dioxide. The ratio of the two molecules is exactly the same as in the atmosphere. It's possible that your planet is covered completely in these protozoa, which stabilize the atmosphere."

"Is that of any significance?"

"Of significance? I don't think so, but it's interesting."

The physicist started on a long litany about the connection between planetary atmospheres and the metabolic processes of living beings, but Russell was no longer listening. He didn't understand any of it anyway. Instead he kept glancing at the clock, hoping that Ellen would return safely.

After the full hour was up she finally returned. She was sweaty and red in the face, but she was well. She greeted the men with a big smile.

"I was on a moon with very low gravitation! Bare, gray rock covered in a powdery dust. No atmosphere. But the mother planet was clear to see in the sky. About twice as big as our moon seen from Earth. It's surrounded by thick clouds, like on photos of Venus or the Saturn moon Titan."

"Why are you out of breath?"

"Nothing to worry about. The cooling system in my suit stopped working. I think one of the valves is blocked. Nothing to worry about. I took some great photos. You'll be very pleased, Dr. Gilbert."

"No sign of civilization or the builders of the transporter?" asked the general, who was standing beside her and helping her to take off her helmet.

"No, I'm afraid not."

"I don't understand," grumbled Morrow. "We've now visited a good dozen destinations, and we haven't found any clues about the constructors. Why are they distributing these spheres in the galaxy if they don't use them? Militarily it makes no sense at all. I would have at least created bases on the more hospitable planets."

"We have to keep searching, General," persisted Gilbert.

"What are you saying? How many possible destinations are there?"

"Well, the configuration mechanism accepts around every second code that we set. That makes about half a trillion possible combinations. Several transporters for every solar system in the Milky Way."

"I fear we could keep on trying for all eternity without finding anything. Half a trillion!" He calculated out loud. "We could do a thousand missions every day and would need more than ten thousand years to visit all of the destinations!"

"We need to be patient," Gilbert reassured him. "At some point we'll come across a clue about who built this thing."

General Morrow turned on his heel and walked off.

"Have you found out anything new about the technology of the sphere?" Russell asked the physicist.

Dr. Gilbert shook his head sadly. "No, nothing. The machine is a big black box for us. We can't find any trace of a mechanism, a power source, or anything else. We can operate the transporter, but that's about it. But we have one more hope."

"Which is?"

"As we discovered, the pressure we feel in our heads is an attempt by the sphere to communicate with us. We need to focus on that now, although we're still waiting for the special equipment and the tomography machines. In the meantime, your people will continue with your missions."

My people?

"Whatever you say, Doc!"

26. Nothing Found

Next day, it was Albert's turn. Like the first time, he showed no sign of nervousness. He grinned and joked before climbing up the steps to the transporter. Half an hour later he returned in one piece. He had materialized in an ocean.

"At first I thought I was weightless. It was only when I looked at the scanner that I realized I was in an aquarium. Half the gravity of Earth. Half a bar of pressure. Then I swam out, but there was only darkness. No life, no sign of the constructors. Nothing."

He handed his scanner to the physicist, but it had given up the ghost in the water. After giving his report he went out with Holbrook.

Next up was Jim. As Gilbert, Russell and Cummings selected the destination for him together from the control pillar, there were a few irritations. For the first time, there was a conflict of opinion.

"Well, I can only feel a slight pressure," said Cummings. Gilbert concurred, only Russell disagreed.

"I don't have one of those throbbing headaches, like with the fatal destinations, but the pressure is considerably worse than the last few days. I think we should select a different destination."

"Are you sure? To me it feels the same as yesterday," said Gilbert. Russell concentrated. Was it a coincidence? Was it just him? Perhaps because he hadn't slept well the night before? But yes, the pressure was stronger.

"I wouldn't risk it. What do you think?" He looked at today's candidate.

Jim was standing beside them in his space suit.

He was also sensitive to the radiation, but not as sensitive as Russell and Gilbert.

"I've only got a slight headache. It doesn't feel any different from yesterday. I think I'll risk it. Maybe this way we'll get a few answers."

"That concludes the matter. Have a safe trip, Mr. Rogers," said General Morrow, who was also standing next to the control pillar.

"Wish me luck, people. See you shortly!" called Jim. He pulled on his helmet and went up the steps to the transporter.

A quarter-of-an-hour later he returned from his mission. As he stepped out of the opening Russell got a big shock. His space suit, which had just been gleaming white, was now black. A few parts of it were completely charred. Jim gasped for air. He was sweating and red in the face. Russell hurried over to him and took off his helmet. It was glowing hot.

"Help me get out of my space suit."

Russell and Colonel Holbrook helped him, until Jim was sitting in his underwear on the bottom step. He was still breathing heavily. Dr. Gilbert checked the portable scanner and whistled through his teeth. Cummings checked Jim and stuck an infrared thermometer in his ear.

"My God, you have temperature of over a hundred-and-four! Where the hell were you, man?"

"In a not very hospitable place, Doctor. I immediately realized that it was very warm. Carbon dioxide atmosphere with around two bar. And a temperature of about seven-hundred-and-fifty degrees Fahrenheit. The cooling system of the suit was on full blast."

"Why didn't you come straight back?" asked

Russell.

"At first the suit seemed to be able to cope with the heat. I didn't even notice it at first. So I wanted to see what it looked like outside."

"You went *outside?*"

"Yes, and that was nearly the end of me. I opened the sphere and was looking straight into hell. It was a barren landscape with a black, smoke-filled sky. Volcanoes spewing lava; red fiery lakes everywhere. One of them was directly in front of the sphere. The thermal radiation from the magma was horrendous. It singed the suit within seconds. I only had the sphere opened for a few seconds, but that was enough. The cooling system stopped working and immediately it was hellishly hot in the suit. I went straight back up to the transporter and came back. I should have listened to you, Russell."

"In future we won't risk selecting that kind of destination. Right, General?" asked Russell emphatically. He turned to look at Morrow, who nodded slowly.

"Agreed."

The following day, Vance Hilmers was the last of the group to make his second trip. He returned safe and sound an hour later. He had been on a bleak and gray planetoid and had taken lots of photos. He told them excitedly about the sky.

"It was fantastic! The Milky Way was an incredibly bright band. But it didn't stretch across the whole sky like it does here, but only across half of the sky. But it was unbelievably bright, particularly in the middle of the band. Apart from that there were hardly any stars in the sky. Far fewer than we can see from Earth. On one side, the sky was almost completely black. Can you explain why that was, Dr. Gilbert?"

"Yes, I presume you were somewhere on the edge of our home galaxy. The stellar population is far lower there. Particularly in the areas between the individual spiral arms. Our sun is situated approximately in the middle of a spiral arm. That's why we can see so many stars from Earth. I'm excited to see your photos. Thank you." He paused briefly to look up longingly at an imaginary sky. "One day I would like to go in the transporter, too."

"That won't happen any time soon," the general said with a frown. "You are far too valuable to us. As long as you're heading the project, I won't allow it."

"But we talked about it. I don't see any danger in travelling to a planetoid like Summers. Our astronauts have already been there dozens of times."

"I don't want to get into this conversation with you," said the general in a raised voice. "My decision is final, Doctor. Do you understand?"

The scientist walked off, grumbling. Engineer Blumberg grinned in amusement.

"There's no need for you to look so amused, Blumberg. Get on with preparing the equipment for the missions this afternoon."

"What are you planning this afternoon?" asked Russell.

"Colonel Holbrook and Lieutenant Redmont will go to your grass planet and carry out further tests. We're planning something interesting."

"Oh?"

"Your samples are very promising. It looks like we can breathe there, and we'll try it out this afternoon. I also requested a drone from the air force, which has now arrived. Holbrook will assemble it on the planet and carry out an aerial reconnaissance via remote control. I can't imagine that there is nothing there but grass. The planet is obviously able to support life. I want to find out whether there are any signs of civilization on the planet."

Russell pricked up his ears. This mission sounded interesting—all the more so because he had discovered it.

"I want to take part in the mission. I want to volunteer."

The general looked at him thoughtfully. "Hm. We have already planned the mission precisely and I don't know what function you could have."

"See it as training."

Morrow considered for a few seconds and then nodded. "Alright, approved. You need to be at the transporter at fourteen-hundred hours."

27. The Drone

"Quite something, your drone."

Russell stood beside two containers the size of wardrobe trunks. He was already wearing his EMU, but hadn't yet put on his helmet. Lieutenant Redmont stood beside him.

"It's easier than it looks. We've made life a bit easier for ourselves by installing a baggage conveyor belt next to the steps."

Two soldiers came over and carried the cases to the sphere.

"Yesterday we also added a conveyor belt, as well as some steps, to the sphere on your planet. It's the first planet on which life has been discovered. And you found it." Redmont grinned at Russell. "That's sure to get your name into the history books. And who knows, perhaps there'll be a settlement there in a few years time, and the whole planet ends up being colonized. They'll put up a statue in your honor."

Russell laughed. "Then don't forget to bring along some pigeons to cover the statue in shit."

"In any case, I'm quite sure we will be visiting the planet often. Once we've verified that the air is breathable, we'll send biologists and other scientists. The exobiologist to whom we sent your samples went wild when he opened the package! He's over the moon!"

Colonel Holbrook came up to them. "Great that you're coming along, Russell. I'm ready. Is everything prepared, Blumberg?"

The engineer nodded.

"Good, then let's go."

The men climbed up the steps and entered the

transporter. Holbrook set the destination code and indicated to Redmont and Russell to put on their helmets.

"Air to ground voice check?"

"Positive. We have radio contact," confirmed Redmont.

"Yes, everything fine," confirmed Russell. "If the air on the planet is breathable, the scientists could also be transported without space suits."

"I don't know," said the colonel. "I wouldn't get into the transporter without a space suit. There have to be a few basic safety measures. Watch out, the transport is about to begin. Three, two, one. And here we are already. Thousands of light years away in the blink of an eye. I still can't get my head around it."

Russell went to the wall and created an opening. Then he grabbed one of the cases and dragged it over to the conveyor belt that had been installed in the outer sphere.

"I wonder how long we'll need to develop this kind of technology for ourselves. Hundreds of years? Thousands? A million? It's frightening, when you think about it."

Redmont started the conveyor belt. Holbrook was already standing at the bottom and lifting the containers off the belt.

"What I can't get my head around," he said, "is that the builders of the spheres have obviously plastered the whole galaxy full of these things—but that might have been millions of years ago. They would have had enough time to colonize the whole Milky Way, but there's no sign of them anywhere. To me that's the biggest mystery of all. I've spent sleepless nights thinking about it, but I can't come up with an explanation."

"Perhaps they destroyed themselves?" speculated Redmont.

"Even if they destroyed one planet, they would have had millions of other planets on which their civilization could have continued to flourish," pointed out Russell.

"Perhaps they came into contact with another civilization, which wiped them out," pondered Redmont.

"That's not convincing either," said Holbrook. "Then this other civilization would have colonized the galaxy. Think about it: we've found a way of using the transporter fairly safely, and are now starting to explore planets in distant solar systems. Think ahead a hundred years—human beings will be colonizing the galaxy thanks to this alien technology. If there were other civilizations in the Milky Way that had come across a transporter, they would have already colonized the galaxy. As far as I'm concerned this can mean only one thing: there are only two superior civilizations in the galaxy—us humans and the mysterious builders of this interstellar transport network. And there's no sign of them. So there you go. Enough speculating. Let's get to work."

The men carried the containers from the outer sphere and laid them outside on the grass. Russell looked again at the strange, surreal landscape. It was like something out of a dream. There was a light breeze, which swirled the alien plants into unusual patterns. The pink-colored sky brought back memories of an LSD trip that he had once been on, way back when in his youth.

Once the cases were unloaded, Holbrook began

to remove his helmet.

"I'll make a start. Watch me carefully. The chemical analyses came out perfectly, and the eggheads couldn't find any trace of spores or other biological dangers, but I'm skeptical. If I collapse make sure that you get me back quickly."

The astronaut began to unfasten his helmet and flipped up the visor. Then he took a deep breath—the first breath a human had taken on another plant.

"The air smells strange. Really weird. But not unpleasant." He took another deep breath and then carried on breathing normally. "It seems to be fine. I feel normal. Right then, you can take off your helmets."

Russell undid the latch, took off his helmet and laid it on the ground. Then he, too, took a deep breath. Holbrook was right, the air smelled strange. It was dry and warm. It reminded him of a long-ago trip to the South of France, where he had walked through endless fields of lavender. The smell was similar.

Then he took off his gloves, kneeled down and ran his hand over the strange grass, and remembered that it wasn't actually even a plant.

What had Gilbert said? What were these things called again? He'd forgotten …

For Russell, it was simply an alien plant life form. It felt like damp grass.

Holbrook opened one of the containers and took out a small airplane. The wings were folded down. He unfolded them, removed some covers to reveal camera lenses and other instruments, and lay the drone down on the ground.

The control unit was in another case and resembled a small laptop. Holbrook placed the remote-control device on a small folding table and switched it on.

"Russell, you can help me. Take the airplane and hold it high up in the air. As soon as I've started the engine with the remote control, throw it forward with force."

"Sure, no problem. I worked with these things in Afghanistan." Russell took the drone and once the propeller started with a loud buzzing, he released it into the air. The little airplane had a wingspan of around six feet and immediately rose into the air.

"Looks good," Holbrook said, satisfied. Crystal-clear images appeared on the screen. "I'll get it up to a cruising altitude of three-thousand feet and then fly it west."

"What's its range?" asked Redmont.

"We can fly it around the whole planet, and that's exactly what we'll do."

"You're kidding me!" cried Redmont. "That thing can't have that much fuel on board."

Russell grinned. He knew the specifications of this system. "The drone doesn't have any fuel, it flies electrically. There's a little RTG in the fuselage which produces the electricity."

"A what?"

"A radioisotope thermoelectric generator. Inside it is a small plutonium tablet. The decay heat of the radioactive material is turned into electricity by thermo-elements. After twenty years there's only about a fifty percent reduction in power."

Holbrook looked at the young astronaut impatiently. "Good God, Redmont. How long have you been an astronaut? They were already using radioisotope generators on the Apollo flights to power their ALSEPs. You should know that!"

The lieutenant looked browbeaten. "Okay, but how do you want to maintain radio contact when it's beyond the horizon? We don't have any satellites to communicate with the drone.

Holbrook looked as if he was about to lose his cool. "Once the short-wave connection is broken off, the drone will of course keep flying automatically. And before you ask about satellite navigation: the drone will navigate itself with the help of a gyrocompass.

"I knew that, Colonel," retorted Redmont churlishly.

"Good, then we've got that cleared."

Russell was enjoying being in the company of these two. Redmont was constantly making gaffes like this and being rebuked by the head astronaut.

After a few hours, there was still no change to be seen in the landscape on the screen. The drone was flying over the same, monotonous hilly green landscape. Meanwhile the men had prepared themselves a meal with a little gas cooker. Holbrook had already switched the airplane to automatic.

Suddenly the radio contact was lost.

"How far away is it now?" asked Russell.

"The drone is flying at around two hundred miles an hour. We've been here for four hours, so around eight-hundred miles."

"I'm starting to think that the physicist is right. The whole planet is covered in this green stuff."

"On earth there are also vast, monotonous areas. Imagine if a Martian landed in the Antarctic and went straight ahead for a hundred miles. It would think the whole of Earth is covered in ice. We'll only know for sure once the drone has scanned the entire planet."

"And what happens next?"

"The drone will fly on automatic once around the planet. Then it will change direction by a few degrees on its own and start the next orbit. It will keep doing this until the whole planet has been scanned. Of course that will take some time and we won't stay here that long. The receiver will record everything and in a few days we, or a colleague, will return to collect the data. Perhaps we'll know more then. I would say that our work is done. We can return to Earth."

That evening Russell, Ellen, Albert, Jim, and Vance Hilmers sat in the rec room. Jim had got ahold of a bottle of bubbly and they celebrated the fact that they had finished the second series of transports without anybody losing their life. Russell told them about his experiences with the astronauts and they discussed their recent missions.

"Your theory about the headaches being a warning sign was pretty fucking good," praised Albert. "Without you, it's unlikely we would have all survived."

"Yeah," agreed Jim, who then turned to look directly at Russell. "I speak on behalf of all of us when I say that we owe you our lives!"

Russell felt uncomfortable. He didn't like it when others felt in his debt.

"Forget about it," he said dismissively. "It was pure self-interest."

Albert noticed Russell's discomfort and changed the subject. "It's strange that we don't all react in the same way to the sphere's *communication* or whatever you want to call it. I always only have a slight headache when I get in the transporter and it always feels the same, whatever the destination."

"For me it's different every time," said Russell. "Depending on the destination it's either a pressure in my head, or a pounding in my temples or behind my forehead. And with the most dangerous destinations it's a pain that permeates my whole brain." He put down his empty glass and went to the icebox to get a can of beer. "I'm annoyed that I didn't notice it before. But when we got to the sphere, Gilbert had usually already set the destination, and after you adjust the code it usually takes a bit of time before the feeling in your head changes. When I came back from the mission today, Cummings was just setting up his computer tomography. He asked me to be his guinea pig tomorrow and to lie in the tube."

"And what does he hope to find out?" asked Ellen.

"I don't know, I guess I'll find out tomorrow."

"And what happens next?" asked Vance. "As far as I know, no further missions are planned. Has the general spoken to you?"

"Yes, very briefly," replied Russell. "He wanted to phone Washington today. There will probably be more missions in a few days. Based on what's happened in the last few days, he presumes that we can use the transporter without much danger. The astronauts have also expressed an interest in being teleported to new destinations."

Ellen snorted. "Yeah, right. Now that the dirty work has been done, they want to play explorer again. Especially the younger ones will be hoping to be the first to make some great new discovery. But I was no different. I know Holbrook. Soon he'll take control and divide up all the missions among his people."

"Then they won't need us anymore. Perhaps we'll be pardoned before the ten missions are up," speculated Hilmers with a hopeful expression.

"Well, I'll accept the pardon and then volunteer for further missions," said Albert.

"Are you crazy?" retorted Hilmers. "Have you become an adrenalin junkie? I want to get out of here as soon as possible."

"I'm a test pilot," explained Albert. "Danger has always been part of my life. And yes, I need the adrenalin rush. I couldn't imagine sitting in an office and sorting through papers. What do you want to do after this is over?"

"I'm going to go to my brother in Florida," answered Hilmers promptly. "He's opened a beach bar on Daytona Beech and it's going well. He'll need my help."

"And what do you intend to do?" Albert asked Russell.

He glanced furtively over at Ellen. She glanced back at him with lowered eyes and smiled.

"To be honest, I haven't thought about it yet. Up to a few days ago I thought I wouldn't get out of here in one piece. But I have to admit that I enjoyed the mission today. Discovering foreign, exotic countries and doing something useful at the same time—that's what I promised myself years ago when I joined the military. I could imagine sticking to it." Russell paused briefly, then added: "I also don't know if I could adjust to an ordinary life out there. I've been a soldier for too long, always on the go."

"You can become a soldier again," said Hilmers.

"And fix the mess our politicians have made? Never again. And what are your plans, Jim?"

"I don't know. There are enough people out there who would like to see me dead because I divulged state secrets. According to them, I'm a traitor to our country." He laughed out loud. "But in fact, I love my country. I just have different ideas from our president. I want an America based on justice and openness. Maybe I'll join an organization that's trying to achieve that. I've been given a new life, and I want to do something useful with it. But I can't imagine carrying on with these transports. Every time I get into that sphere I think I'm about to have a heart attack. Just thinking about being teleported makes me tense up. I'm not an adventurer. There are others who are better suited to that kind of life than me. I'm going to take the first opportunity I get to get out of here."

He turned to Ellen. "And I bet we can guess what our astronaut wants to do?"

Ellen grinned at him. "Yup! I'll stay here and work as an astronaut again. I've already spoken to Holbrook and he's going to try and help me get reaccepted by the Astronaut Corps."

Russell nodded. It was just what he had expected. He liked the idea of discovering new worlds with Ellen. But could she really imagine a future together with him? They had gotten together during the early stage of this surreal project, because they didn't want to confront death on their own. But in the last few days that danger had disappeared. Would her feelings for him remain the same, now that she had a future? They hadn't spoken about it yet. Everything had moved too fast in the last few days. He also realized that he was afraid of talking it over with her. But at some point they would have to.

28. Tomography

"Do you suffer from claustrophobia?" asked Doctor Cummings.

"No, why?" asked Russell.

"Some people have problems being in the narrow tube. I would have given you a mild sedative."

"Don't worry. Just tell me what you're going to do."

Russell stood in the cave. The technicians had set up a tomography machine some distance away from the sphere. It consisted of a seven-foot-long tube. He sat down on a stretcher that stuck out of the thick metal cylinder.

"We're going to do a scan outside the sphere to record your normal brain activity. Then we'll set up the machine in the sphere, to compare it to your brain activity under the influence of radiation."

"I was once in an MRI scanner after I was wounded in Afghanistan. I didn't realize you could also measure brain activity with it."

"MRI scanner is just an acronym. The correct term is magnetic resonance imaging scanner."

Smart-ass.

"We're going to use a procedure called fMRT. The f stands for functional. Activated areas of the brain have an increased blood flow, which the tomography machine recognizes as a change in the percentage of oxygenated hemoglobin. The machine makes very short scans and immediately compares them on the computer. If there is a change in brain activity, it's indicated on the screen by different colors. We want to know which areas of your brain are activated through your communication with the sphere.—Here. Put on these headphones." Cummings handed him a pair. "Depending on the sequence, the machine can be very loud and with these we can continue to talk. Do you have any tattoos?"

"No, why?"

"The oscillating magnetic fields would induce heat in the metallic pigments and burn your skin. Now please lie down."

Russell lay down on the stretcher, which was driven into the cylinder by the doctor. The tube was very narrow. The scan began and Russell could hear loud metallic clicking sounds.

"Relax. Try not to think of anything in particular. Have you ever meditated?"

"Yes, quite intensively in fact. It helped me in Afghanistan."

"Good. Then meditate now."

Russell emptied his mind. He pushed aside any thoughts or images until he was overcome by that familiar, almost out-of-body feeling. Now and again images floated into his mind, but he gently nudged them away. He lost all sense of time. Finally the time was up and the stretcher was pulled back out of the tube.

"Well, Doctor. How does it look in my brain?"

The medic smiled. "Completely normal. You're good at meditation. There were hardly any fluctuations in your brain activity. Perfect reference material. You can get up. The technicians will now disassemble the machine and take it to the sphere. It will take a while."

"Then let's go and have a coffee."

"No, please not. The stimulants would induce

increased activity in some parts of the brain. Since we want to compare the images of your brain in the sphere with those outside, coffee would distort the results."

"Okay. I'll go and sit over there and wait."

"Thanks, Russell."

It took longer than expected for the two technicians to set up the tomography machine in the sphere. Finally Cummings called him over. Dr. Gilbert had joined him.

"While you lie in the machine, we will select various known destinations on the console, to see if we can recognize any sign of pressure in your head on the fMRT output. I won't talk to you in order not to distract you. Just try and clear your mind again."

As he was driven into the machine on the stretcher, Russell felt the familiar headache again. A destination hadn't been set, so that he only felt a slight pressure. He tried to relax again and to think of nothing in particular. But it was harder than it had been outside the sphere. He pushed aside any thoughts, but images kept flashing in his mind and then disappearing again. Deep inside him he could hear Ellen's voice and presumed it was a memory floating up to the surface of his consciousness. He pulled himself together and tried to suppress the voice.

Concentrate. Don't let yourself be distracted.

But it didn't really work. Why not? He was so experienced in meditation, he had been able to use it in the most difficult of situations, but now it simply wouldn't work. He was annoyed with himself.

Suddenly he was overcome by a strong, pounding headache. He had a feeling of danger, fear and despair.

Gilbert has changed the destination. I can feel it.

Eventually the headache and unpleasant feelings subsided, until he could only feel a light pressure and a strange tingling sensation—as if someone was fumbling around with his head. And he kept thinking he could hear the distant voice of Ellen, although he couldn't understand what she was trying to tell him.

With a sudden jolt, the stretcher was pulled back out of the cylinder and the scan was over.

Russell looked into the amazed faces of Dr. Cummings and Dr. Gilbert.

"Well Doctors? Was it helpful?"

Dr. Cummings fiddled nervously with the pen in his hand. "I've never seen anything like it. Come and have a look at the screen."

Russell went over to the screen and looked at the three-dimensional, gray image of a brain. His brain.

"This here is your brain activity outside of the sphere."

A video was played and Russell could see parts of his brain occasionally light up blue before the color faded again.

"That was your normal state during your meditation. Hardly any activity. All quite normal. And now look at this."

Suddenly his whole brain was a deep red color. Some parts turned to yellow and then back to a deep red.

"What does it mean?"

"It means your brain is working like crazy. The colors show the change in blood flow, which are normal in brain activity. Depending on what you're thinking, or what task your brain is working on, particular parts of the brain light up red—first here, and then there. But here your whole brain is active."

"And you think that's because of the sphere?"

"Yes, it's doing something to your brain. You can also produce this effect artificially. I know about it from a trans-cranial magnetic stimulation, which is used for some illnesses. It explains the headaches and the pressure in your head. The radiation being emitted by the sphere has the same effect. Just much stronger."

Russell shook his head. This was going over his head.

"You said the sphere is doing something with my brain?" he asked after a pause. "What is it doing? Is it dangerous?"

"I don't know. By God, I don't know. I don't think it's dangerous in the sense of causing cancer or injuries. But the sphere is firing up your neurons and that's influencing the formation of synapses."

Russell was at a loss. "And what now? Does that mean I should stay away from the sphere?"

"No, I wouldn't go that far. I see it as an unsuccessful attempt to establish communication with us. The alien builders of the sphere must have had completely different brains. Do you see? Perhaps they didn't have any mouths or ears, but talked to each other telepathically. It's fantastic! I wouldn't have thought something like that was possible"

Russell left the outer sphere and was still at a loss. Outside, General Morrow came toward him.

"Good morning, Harris. I was just on my way to see you. Were they able to find anything out?"

"Ask the doctors in there. They're pretty excited."

The general laughed and shook his head. "They've been pretty excited ever since we brought them this alien machine. Sometimes I think that Gilbert sees the transporter as his personal toy. But it was the same with the Manhattan Project. Oppenheimer regarded the atomic bomb as his baby. But after Hiroshima and Nagasaki he wanted us to give him back his toy. These nerds will never get to grips with reality. I'll talk to Cummings later."

"Do you know yet how it's going to continue?"

"Yes, I spoke with the Pentagon yesterday. The transports to unknown destinations will continue in a few days. But there will be a few changes."

"What kind of changes?"

"For one thing, our regular astronauts will also select new destinations."

"You mentioned that already. And the other thing?"

"In the future, you won't travel alone anymore, but in teams of two or three."

Russell couldn't hide his surprise. "Oh?"

"The new method of judging the danger of the destination seems to be reliable. In light of this new situation, I think it is appropriate to send teams whose members can help one another. You will also have more freedom in choosing your missions. You can all choose when and with whom you want to go on a mission. But the agreed ten missions per person still stands. In two months you will all be free."

"That's great news."

"I guessed you'd be pleased. What's more, I would like to offer you the opportunity to continue working for us after the ten missions have been completed. Think about it."

Russell didn't need to think about it. He'd made up his mind a while ago.

That same evening, he and Ellen decided to go on the next mission together. Morrow set the date for two days later. The following morning, Russell drove down to the cave to check his space suit. Apart from that there was nothing more for him to do.

He stopped in front of the container where the suits were kept and looked around. There were more people than usual in the cave. Men and women in combat uniforms were unloading pieces of equipment from a truck and stacking them up next to the sphere. Something was going on.

At that moment, Colonel Holbrook stepped out of the transporter. He was still wearing his space suit, and had his helmet tucked under his arm. Russell went up to him.

"I've just returned from your planet. I downloaded the recordings made by the drone."

"Well? Did it find anything interesting?"

The astronaut shook his head. "Nothing. The whole damn planet is covered in that green stuff. Whichever way you look, the same hilly landscapes covered in that strange grass. No mountains, no rivers, no oceans. I reprogrammed the course of the drone. It's now flying north over the pole. But I doubt it will find anything new. The temperature is also interesting. All over the planet it's exactly seventy-nine-point-three degrees Fahrenheit. It doesn't vary by even a tenth of a degree. Even on the dark side."

"It doesn't even cool down at night? How is that possible?"

"I have no idea. Maybe it has to do with that green stuff. Damn, there's so much to learn and so many worlds to discover. We need more scientists and real explorers. An international team would be best—like on the ISS. With top experts from every country."

"Then you should do that."

"Oh, there's no chance of that happening as long as this damn project is top secret. We have to work with military scientists, and General Morrow doesn't intend to change that in the foreseeable future." He looked around to see if anyone else was in earshot, before continuing: "We haven't seen eye to eye on this from the start. In my opinion, this teleportation machine doesn't belong in the hands of the military. I think a civilian organization should be established to administer it, in the same way that NASA managed the Apollo program. But Morrow still thinks he might discover some superior weapons technology, and he doesn't want the Chinese to get their hands on it. And our stupid President would rather throw the transporter back in the ocean than share it with another nation." He sighed. "Unfortunately I have no say in the matter. And as for you, it's back to work tomorrow ..."

"Yes, Ellen and I will be the first team. We set off tomorrow."

Holbrook nodded. "I'll be checking out a new destination with Redmont the day after you."

"The general calls it *scouting.*"

"I don't care what he calls it. But it's definitely time for us real astronauts to go on a proper mission again. We can't leave it all to you amateurs."

Russell laughed but quickly became serious.

"What are all these people doing here?"

Holbrook shrugged. "Morrow's idea. He wants to establish a base on the grass planet. Thirty men and women are going in the transporter today and will be setting up a base over the next few weeks."

"But it sounds like there isn't much to find there."

"Morrow regards it as training. He wants to see how they handle a mission with the transporter. And there are military scientists from Los Alamos among them: atmospheric researchers, biologists and astronomers. They'll be carrying out research there. The station on the Summers planetoid is now permanently inhabited. There are four scientists stationed there. The program is slowly gaining momentum."

29. Encounter

The following day, Russell and Ellen checked the equipment in the transporter one last time. Ellen entered the destination code that they had selected earlier and considered to be safe. This was another new development. From now on they were allowed to start the transporter alone. Gilbert, who was a bit of a control freak, had not been happy about this decision, but eventually he had yielded.

"Right, I think we're all set," said Ellen. "Ready?"

Russell closed his eyes and concentrated. He could feel a slight pressure in his head. He thought he could hear a quiet voice again, but he could be imagining it.

"Good to go!"

Ellen held his hand, and with her other hand she pressed the field on the console.

Russell didn't notice any change. But still he let go of Ellen's hand and looked at his scanner.

"Close to Earth's gravity. Atmosphere 1.2 bar. Temperature 59 degrees Fahrenheit."

"Check the atmospheric composition."

Russell adjusted his device.

"Nitrogen 75 percent. Oxygen 22 percent. Carbon dioxide 0.02 percent. The rest are inert gases. Almost the same as Earth."

"Looks like we've found another Earth-like planet. Let's go out and look."

They made an opening in the outer sphere and lowered themselves down on the ropes. Then they lumbered over to the outer wall in their space suits. Russell raised his hand and made an opening.

"Oh wow!" gasped Ellen.

Russell, too, was overwhelmed. The sphere was on a carpet of grass. There were bushes and trees. Huge tree trunks towered over them.

"Gees, take a look at that!" exclaimed Russell. "They're enormous! At least half a mile high!"

The trees looked like gigantic pine trees, but with a strange, leathery skin. The trunks were unusually wide. They towered upward like skyscrapers. The canopy of leaves was hundreds of feet above them, and very dense. They couldn't see the sky—even though the gigantic trees were relatively spread out. The ground glittered with dew and yielded underfoot like moss.

"Incredible," murmured Ellen. She rummaged in her bag, took out her camera and shot some photos.

Russell tapped her on the helmet. "Shall we risk it?"

Ellen considered for a moment and then nodded. "Yeah, why not?"

He undid the latch on his helmet and carefully took it off. He could breathe quite normally.

"It even smells like Earth," he said. "Like a completely normal day in the forest. Let's have a picnic!"

"Can't," said Ellen, who had meanwhile also taken off her helmet. "I forgot the picnic blanket at home."

"Let's take off our suits."

"Why?"

Russell stood in front of Ellen and kissed her gently. "Why do you think?"

She nodded and returned his kisses passionately.

They helped each other out of their heavy suits and made love on the moss-covered ground of an alien planet.

"Do you think we could make a go of it?" asked Russell, running his hand softly over her body. They were lying naked next to each other on the carpet of moss.

"I don't know. I hadn't really ever thought about the future, but in the last few days it's been on my mind. I haven't had the prospect of a normal relationship for such a long time. Not since Steve became ill. I don't know, to be honest. Let's take it slowly and we'll see how things develop. Okay?"

"Okay." He smiled at her.

A cracking sound nearby startled him.

"What was that?" he asked.

"I heard it too. It came from over there." They stood up and Russell looked in the direction that Ellen had pointed. "There! Can you see it?" she whispered nervously.

Russell saw it. It was as big as a German Shepard and had four thickset legs, which carried a massive torso. The body was covered in a brown, leathery skin.

"Oh, God. It's an animal."

"Yes," she breathed.

The creature was about three-hundred feet away and stood stock still.

"Jesus, that thing doesn't have a head!"

The creature looked thoroughly alien—and frightening. It seemed be staring at them, but there were no eyes to be seen on its body. Nothing, in fact, that resembled a sensory organ.

"And we're standing here naked. Do you think it's dangerous?"

"I have no idea," said Russell. "Let's go back to the transporter. If it moves in our direction, we'll run. I wouldn't be surprised if it could move very fast."

They edged backward to the sphere, but the alien being continued to stand stock still and appeared to be waiting. Then it suddenly turned around and ran off.

"Jesus, did you see how fast that thing was?"

Ellen nodded.

"Let's put our suits back on. We shouldn't carry on looking around unarmed."

"I guess you're right."

Russell put his space suit back on and was glad that he didn't have to run back to the transporter naked. He couldn't help grinning at the thought. It would have been a tricky one to explain if they'd returned to Earth naked. Not to mention that it would have been incredibly embarrassing.

They gathered their equipment and travelled back to Earth.

General Morrow was standing in front of the transporter to welcome them back. Russell and Ellen told him about the world they had discovered. When they got to the part about the strange animal, the general listened attentively.

"And it really didn't have a head?" asked Morrow.

"No. There were no bodily orifices to be seen," said Ellen.

"Did you take any photos?"

"No, we were too shocked, and then it disappeared again quickly," explained Russell.

The general shrugged. "No problem. We'll be

able to see it on the recordings of your helmet cameras."

"Um, we'd switched off the helmet cameras."

The general looked surprised. "Why, Mr. Harris?"

"We'd taken off our helmets."

"Without waiting for any further analyses?" Now the general sounded annoyed.

It occurred to Russell that he hadn't actually switched off his helmet camera. He mustn't forget to delete the memory card.

Who knows what's on it? In the worst-case scenario, the first ever interstellar porn movie. Holy shit.

Judging by the expression on her face, Ellen was having the same thought.

"We thought it was safe. The scanner didn't identify any chemical or biological dangers."

"Next time you need to stick to the rules! What else did you find?"

"Nothing. Just forest. If the trees had been smaller it could have been on Earth."

"I would like a more thorough analysis of this planet to be carried out," said Morrow decisively and turned to his right. "Colonel Holbrook?"

"Sir?"

"Get us another drone. If there is life on that planet, it might find signs of civilization."

"It won't be able to gain height in that forest. We need to find an open space or a clearing that's big enough for it to take off."

"Well, in that case it's time for an expedition! Put together equipment for two days. You and Lieutenant Redmont will set off tomorrow. Do you want to go with them, Harris?"

"Yes, definitely."

"I'll go too," said Ellen.

"Okay, that should be a big enough team. I'll provide a carrier robot to take the drone. You can leave your space suits here. Obviously you don't need them."

Holbrook didn't look happy about this instruction. "Do you think that's wise?"

"The space suits will only hinder you. We think the destination is safe. You'll depart tomorrow at 0800 hours. I want some answers."

30. Mission

Soldiers had already taken the necessary equipment to the transporter. This included a four-legged horse-size robot from Seattle Labs and a conveyer belt to install on the foreign planet. The expedition members were in green combat uniforms. From behind, Russell could hear the voice of the general. When he turned around he got a surprise. Morrow, who almost always wore his formal staff uniform, was also in combat gear.

"What's all this about, General? You don't want to …?"

"I'm coming with you and taking over command of the mission. I want to finally see something for myself."

"Have you discussed this with the Pentagon?"

The general grinned—which happened rarely. "They don't need to know, Harris."

"You'll get into trouble."

"Not serious trouble. I was never told not to get in the transporter, so I'm not violating any orders. Enough talking. Is everyone ready?"

"Yes, we can go."

"Alright then, let's do it."

They climbed into the transporter. Holbrook programmed the destination and checked the settings. Clearly he was not happy about being teleported without a pressure suit, but he had to follow the general's orders. A minute later, they were on an alien planet, light years away from Earth.

"It's certainly incredible," said the general, impressed. "You don't even notice that you're being transported."

Holbrook and Redmont set up the conveyor belt on the outside of the transporter and together they brought the equipment outside. Morrow started the four-legged robot, which was already carrying the equipment and the drone on its load area. It was programmed to follow the general at a distance of about ten feet. When it moved on its high-tech legs, you could hear a metallic whirring and the hissing of pneumatic valves.

"That thing is pretty quiet. How is it powered?" asked Russell.

"The first models were powered with a combustion engine. But that was too loud for many missions. That's why the new generation has an inbuilt radioisotope thermoelectric generator. So it works using nuclear electricity."

Holbrook poked Redmont in the ribs and grinned. The lieutenant pulled a face, and looked offended. *I know how drones work!* he seemed to be screaming at his boss. Obviously he hadn't forgotten all the questions he'd asked on the grass planet.

"Where do we go from here?" Holbrook asked.

"We'll march in this direction until it gets dark," ordered the general and indicated the way with his arm. "How long until sunset?"

"We don't have any data for that," explained the colonel. "As long as all we can see is that canopy of leaves up there, we can't know how long a day lasts here, or what the local time is."

"Well, we'll find out."

They set off. Slowly they walked through the trees, whose trunks were as thick as houses. Apart from the noise they were making themselves, they were surrounded by complete and utter silence. There was also nothing to be seen of the headless animals; nonetheless, the general had ordered that the whole group be armed. Each of them was carrying an automatic rifle on their back and a pistol in their holster.

"It's certainly strange," said Holbrook. "Apart from the proportions of the trees, it looks like a forest on Earth. Even the physiology of the plants appears to be similar. A biologist would probably be able to tell us more."

Russell caught up with General Morrow, who was marching on ahead. "What's going on here, General?"

Morrow turned his head and frowned at him. "What do you mean?"

"Why the risk? We don't know anything about this world. We have no idea if there are dangerous animals or other dangers. Why the rush with this long expedition?"

"Oh, Harris. You have no idea. Both the Pentagon and the White House are applying an enormous amount of pressure. We need to find some answers!"

"And you think you might find the answers on this specific planet?"

"There's life here. You saw the animals yourself. Where are they, actually?" He peered between the tree trunks before turning back to Russell. "Anyway, I'm sure I'll get to see them soon enough. But it's possible that we might also find intelligent life here—and traces of civilization. Or are you of a different opinion, Harris?"

"We haven't even seen a fraction of the planets that the transporter can take us to. There could be millions of planets like this one. With life, but without intelligence. And without any sign of the transporter's builders."

The general frowned. "If that's the case, I'm done for."

"What do you mean?"

"You don't need to know everything, Harris."

Russell looked at him with narrowed eyes.

What's he hiding? Is there some secret I don't know about?

He had completed many missions with General Morrow in the past. At the time he had still been a colonel. Russell had never really figured out his superior, but he trusted him. Morrow had an instinct for making the right decisions. He was always fair and loyal toward his men and had never sacrificed one of them in order to distinguish himself. On the contrary. When they had been in the Sudan together, Morrow had adamantly refused to follow the Commander in Chief's order to send a reconnaissance patrol into a valley that was under the control of extremists. Instead, the air force had purged the valley, for which Russell had been incredibly grateful. The patrol would not have had a chance of making it back in one piece. Even back then, Morrow had been pretty self-contained. He'd obviously become more so. But Russell sensed that the general was struggling with something.

After several hours' march through the tree trunks, the small group reached the edge of the forest. In front of them was a grassy meadow that stretched out for about half a mile. Beyond it there was a steep drop.

They walked to the edge of the cliff and looked

down. About a hundred miles below them, another grassy landscape stretched into the distance.

A river meandered its way through the flatland before merging into the distant horizon. To the left, the hills became higher the further you looked, until they segued into a mountain range whose peaks were hidden in swathes of cloud.

Behind them they could finally see just how tall the enormous trees were. The sight was breathtaking.

"The trees must be a mile high," said Ellen in astonishment. "How can they even carry their own weight? They're thirty feet wide at most—that doesn't seem like enough. And this view!" She looked across the vast green expanse with shining eyes.

"Hey, what are those things up there?" Redmont pointed at the sky. At first Russell thought they were clouds, but he was wrong. They were too round for clouds and had distinct outlines.

"Those are living beings!" cried Ellen in amazement. "They're enormous!"

Russell followed the creatures with his eyes. Like gigantic balloons with leathery, brown skin, a good dozen of the alien creatures drifted past high up in the sky.

"I'm guessing they have a diameter of at least a thousand feet, maybe more," he said.

"How can they float like that?" asked Redmont in disbelief.

He got his answer from Holbrook.

"It's only a guess, but I think they work like hot-air balloons. Somehow the sun generates high temperatures inside them. The difference in pressure enables them to fly. It could be that they feed on microorganisms that live in the clouds. They comb the atmosphere like whales on the search for plankton."

"What do they do when there's no sun?" asked Ellen.

"I assume they come down to earth. Spend the night on the ground and take off again at first light."

Russell had to smile. Holbrook was obviously having fun exploring this strange world.

The colonel walked over to a fallen tree. Although the trunk was lying on its side, it was still three times taller than the astronaut. He stood in front of it and started scraping off some of the bark with a knife. Russell strolled over to him.

"Take a look at this!" It was gleaming beneath Holbrook's knife. "It's metal!"

Russell looked at the bark more closely. It was crisscrossed with fine threads of metal in a honeycomb structure.

"The trees must secrete the metal in their resin—and then it accumulates in the bark," Holbrook explained in excitement. "It probably forms as the tree grows. The honeycomb structure supports the tree. Now we know the secret of its height. Without the metal the trees wouldn't be able to carry their own weight. Incredible!"

The general crossed his arms. "With all due respect to your scientific curiosity, Holbrook, we have more important things to do. Please work out when it will get dark and then put the drone into operation as soon as possible."

"Yes Sir."

The astronaut took a kind of sextant from his bag and pointed it at the sun, which was still high in the sky.

"About 0.25 degrees per minute. That means a day lasts about as long as it does on Earth. The sun is still around thirty degrees from the horizon, which gives us another two hours until sunset. We can get the drone started, but we won't make it back to the transporter before nightfall."

"Okay," said the general and gave further orders. "Holbrook and Redmont, you activate the drone. Harris and I will prepare the camp. Miss Slayton, you can put up the tents."

The others went off to carry out the general's orders.

"Harris, I suggest we create a safety zone with a radius of a hundred-and-fifty feet around the picket," said Morrow. "The luggage robot has everything on-board that we need for a safe camp."

"Barbwire and mines?" said Russell with a grin. It was like being back in the Sudan.

"Yes, Harris. Get going. You take care of the mines and I'll deal with the barbwire."

The general made two circles of barbwire around the camp. In between, Russell buried mines with proximity sensors. They could be activated via radio command. Then anything that came any closer than a thousand feet was dead.

They were finished by sunset. As darkness fell, the stars became visible in the sky. As a soldier he had learned to use them for orientation, but he couldn't see a single familiar constellation. He asked himself how many light years away from Earth they were. After searching in vain for an answer in the stars, he took his backpack and moved to go over to the tent into which Ellen had disappeared, but the general stopped him.

"Give the lady a little privacy. You can share a tent with me. I wanted to talk to you anyway."

Russell would have rather quartered himself with Ellen, but he was curious to hear what Morrow had to say.

31. General Morrow

The camp was finished within an hour. In the meantime, Holbrook had assembled the drone and sent it off. He had programmed a course rather setting it to automatic.

They cooked stew on a gas fire and to everyone's surprise, General Morrow pulled some whisky out of his backpack, which he passed around the group.

The stuff was darn strong. Russell looked at the label. He didn't recognize it, but he presumed it had cost an arm and a leg. After passing the bottle to the next person, he peered out into the darkness.

"I wonder why we haven't seen another one of those creatures."

"Perhaps there aren't many of them," conjectured Ellen. "Or they're shy. The one we saw disappeared pretty quickly. And in this big group, we're making enough noise to warn them off."

"Could be," murmured Russell and placed a finger on his lips thoughtfully.

"There don't seem to be many creatures on this planet in general," said Redmont with emphasis. "Up to now we've only seen those balloon birds. No insects. And I can't hear anything, either."

"A biologist could probably tell us more about the ecology of this planet," said Holbrook. "He would …"

"I'm sure scientists will come and visit this planet soon enough!" the general interrupted him, irritably. "But it doesn't have to be today."

Russell lay on top of his sleeping bag. General Morrow rolled up beside him and they shared the last of the golden liquid in the bottle.

But Russell already felt like he'd had a drop too much, and paced himself. The general, on the other hand, didn't hold back and downed the whiskey in big, greedy gulps.

"Harris, back then I considered you my best man, and I'm glad you're with me on this mission too."

"I feel the same, General. If it wasn't for this project, I would be dead by now."

"You also could have died in the transporter like O'Brien and the others."

"But I didn't."

"No, you didn't," replied the general with a heavy tongue.

"How did you get involved with this project, General?"

Morrow hesitated before replying.

"It's complicated. I think the last time we saw each other was at the Zero-G training?"

"Yes, after that I was detailed to Afghanistan."

"Oh yeah, that's right. I would have prevented it if I could have."

Russell's mind wandered.

Would Karen still be alive if I hadn't been part of that damn mission? At least she wouldn't have been driving to the airport on that fateful night. Goddammit! But these thoughts won't get me anywhere. I shouldn't indulge in them.

"I also would have preferred to stay in your unit than go through that shit in Afghanistan," Russell admitted.

"I can imagine," replied the general. "It must have been the worst."

"I've got nothing against difficult missions, but in

Afghanistan I never had the feeling we were achieving anything worthwhile. And it sucks to risk your life for nothing."

"You don't think your fight against the Taliban made the world a safer place?"

"Not in the way we imagined. We were sent to a Taliban gathering that we were supposed to smoke out. We blew the building up with a drone, but when the dust had settled we realized that the gathering had been a wedding. In the inquiry it came out that our Afghan informant had a private vendetta against the family. And that kind of thing happened constantly. We haven't made the world a safer place. On the contrary; we've created the next generation of terrorists who will thank us over the next twenty years for killing their parents. No, General. I don't want to have anything more to do with our country's wars."

"This project is more appealing, I take it."

"Yes. The thought alone that we're thousands of light years from Earth is fantastic. Now that we've learned how to use the transporter relatively safely, it's starting to be fun. Who knows how many worlds it will open up to us?"

"That's true. But it's even more important that we maintain access to the builders' technology. And that needs to happen as quickly as possible."

"I don't know if we can really influence that. And why the hurry?"

"Because otherwise my head will roll."

Now it's getting interesting.

"What do you mean?"

"I was a good Colonel. None of my missions failed."

"I know that, Sir. That was one of the reasons

why we trusted you."

"Anyhow. After that, they wanted to promote me to general and bring me to the Pentagon. Unfortunately politics isn't my forte—I made a lot of enemies. I always wanted to prove that an army can be commanded for the good of our country and of the occupied country. I was always of the opinion that soldiers who are treated with respect will treat the enemy and foreign civilians humanely. But the growth of technology in our armies is changing things. We already have drones that carry out air strikes, next we'll also have armies of robots on the ground. That transport robot out there can just as easily be equipped with weapons."

"I have to admit, I find the idea frightening."

"I think the best protection for our soldiers is not to send them out into the field anymore. With an army of autonomous robots nobody would attack us anymore."

"Autonomous? You mean they won't even be remote-controlled?"

"Yes. I advocated strongly for this technology. And that was my mistake."

"What do you mean?"

"We deployed a company of robots in Somalia to flush out a group of bandits. It was a joint operation with the CIA and I was in command. We wanted to prove how effective autonomous fighting machines can be for this kind of work. The robots were programmed to identify who was carrying a weapon and to eliminate them. Then they were supposed to secure the location until a special unit was sent in."

"Was the mission a success?"

"It was a disaster. The machines eliminated the

civilian population. Dozens of women and children were in the village. Everyone holding something in their hand was judged to be carrying a weapon. Even a little girl holding a doll in her hand! In the end the bandits were able to immobilize the machines."

"And then?"

"The President wanted to avoid losing face, like that time in Mogadishu. The public wasn't allowed to get wind of it. The Air Force was commanded to bomb the whole town. After that I was a nobody at the Pentagon and I was ridiculed."

"So how did you get to be involved in this project?"

"When the sphere was hauled out of the water off the coast of California, I did everything to get the job. It wasn't even that difficult, so many others thought it was too hot to handle. For me, it was the last chance to end my military career with dignity. But if we can't show any results soon, the project will be handed over to NASA. The President knows that it will be impossible to keep it secret for much longer. Once the public finds out about it, I'll have failed again. In that case I'll end my career a laughing stock. But I assure you—I won't let that happen."

32. Escape

Russell woke up as something bumped into his tent. He could hear Ellen's voice.

"Come out, quick!" she whispered.

Russell woke up the general, who grumbled in annoyance.

"Damn it, what's the matter?"

"I don't know, but something's wrong."

Russell pulled on a shirt and opened the zipper of his tent.

Dawn was breaking so that he could see nearby forest silhouetted against the sky. It was cool and the air was moist, and immediately he started to shiver. Ellen stood next to her tent and stared into the dim light.

Jesus, what is that?

Now he, too, could see the headless, dog-like creatures that they had spotted on their first mission to the planet. Dozens of them were standing around their camp. And more and more were joining them.

Holbrook and Redmont emerged from their tents and saw the creatures, too.

Russell felt a breath in his ear.

"What do they want?" whispered Morrow.

"I don't know. But they seem to be pack animals. A creature on its own hightails it and gets reinforcement. Now the reinforcement is here, I think we're in for some trouble."

The general made a grumbling noise. "They won't get in thanks to the barbwire, but we also can't get out."

Holbrook hurried over to them. "I don't know what they're planning, but we need to react quickly."

"There are a lot of them," Russell pointed out.

"If they decide to attack, the defense ring won't be much use."

Most of the animals stood stock still, around six-hundred feet away. More and more were coming out of the forest.

"Take a light backpack and arm yourselves," ordered the general. "We may have to escape quickly."

"How far is it to the transporter?" asked Russell.

Holbrook had left a radio navigation transmitter at the transporter and looked at the receiver, which he was wearing on his wrist.

"Three miles," he said. "If we run, we can be there in half an hour."

"That's a long way, when you've got a pack of wolves running after you," murmured Ellen.

"The worst thing is, we have no idea what these creatures are capable of," responded the colonel. "They don't have a head, much less recognizable mouths or teeth. How on earth do they eat?"

"One of them is coming closer!" hissed Redmont, who had turned around.

Russell also turned to look the other way. One of the animals was trotting purposefully toward the barbwire. Its movements were lithe as a tiger's.

"What's he planning to do?" whispered Ellen. "It looks as if he wants to go straight through the wire."

As the animal came in contact with the safety wire, the metal melted like butter in the sun. A gray liquid was all that remained of the wire—it dripped down the side of the creature.

"Jesus Christ!" hissed Redmont. "They secrete acid from their skins. I don't believe it!"

"Watch out, it's nearly at the mines!" warned

Russell.

As the ground exploded beneath the creature there was a loud bang. Red liquid and brown tissue sprayed in every direction. As if on signal, the other animals now approached the camp.

"Shit. Run!" cried Russell. "Through the gap in the minefield and back to the transporter!"

He shot at some of the animals that were standing beyond the gap in the minefield. They immediately keeled over and were dead.

"Go! Now!" yelled Morrow.

They ran through the gap and into the forest, the animals hot on their heels.

"Shoot, goddammit!" screamed Holbrook, stopping at the edge of the forest to fire at the approaching animals. Some of the creatures fell to the ground. Those right behind stopped for a moment, before spurting forward again.

"Run, for Christ's sake!" cried the general and kept running. "We can't stand up to this attack. More keeping coming!"

They ran in a tight formation toward the transporter. Russell shot at the animals that came too close to him.

"They're surrounding us. Damn!" cried Redmont.

Russell noticed that a few of the creatures were running past him to the side. Soon they would be approaching from the front.

As they ran, Redmont kept turning around to shoot. Consequently, he didn't notice a big root. He got caught on it with his shoe and fell to the ground.

"Redmont!" screamed Russell and wanted to shoot the animals behind him, but it was too late.

One of the creatures was bending over him. It lowered its body onto Redmont's chest, which immediately started to dissolve with a loud hissing noise. The lieutenant screamed in agony. Blood and a white liquid ran down his side. Some of it was absorbed by the animal's skin. Redmont was still screaming. Blood and saliva were spluttering from his mouth.

Russell shot at the beast. It fell backward, but there was barely anything left of Redmont's chest and his screams died away with a final rattle.

"Harris! Come on!" shouted the general.

The others had already run ahead and Russell caught up with them. He kept on firing at the animals behind him. If it carried on like this he would soon run out of ammunition.

As the sphere finally came into view, he was completely out of breath. Dozens of animals had gotten within several feet of him. Luckily, the creatures weren't as fast as Russell had initially feared. But they couldn't have run much further.

Russell shot at the rapidly approaching creatures, while Holbrook opened the sphere. Russell was the last to go through the opening backward, and he almost tripped. Then the colonel closed the opening and they were safe.

"Fuck!" swore the general.

Anger was welling up in Russell, too, although his was directed toward his commander. The old Morrow would never have embarked on a kamikaze mission like this. The political games in the Pentagon had corrupted him and the mission in Somalia had tipped the general over the edge.

I can't trust his judgment anymore.

33. Contact

That evening, Russell lay in bed next to Ellen. He was still furious and had talked himself into a rage.

"I'm starting to agree with Holbrook. This project belongs in civilian hands! Morrow is desperate for results in order to clear his name. That'll cost us our lives!"

"And what do you want to do about it?"

"Nothing. But I'm still livid about this failed mission. We should have set up camp next to the transporter and slowly gone out to explore the area. Redmont's death was totally pointless. And we won't be able to access the data from the drone without sending out a commando. I doubt there's any civilization on the planet, in any case. If there was, the sphere wouldn't have ended up in the middle of a forest. It was one almighty screw-up!"

"Until recently, you were full of praise for the general."

"When I was in his unit, we never set out without detailed planning. There was always a retreat route. Morrow would try and minimize the danger, and if a mission seemed too risky, he would fight it out with his superiors. He was always responsible and loyal toward his men. But I'm afraid that all that's left of that Morrow is a façade."

"What's going to happen now?"

"What do you think? We're going to check another destination every day until we find something."

"You don't think that's the right strategy?"

"I think we'll still be going on daily searches for new worlds in fifty years' time, without finding any sign of the constructers. There are just too many destinations. But there aren't really any alternatives. Maybe Gilbert will find out something about how the sphere works or Cummings will discover something with his tomographies."

"Have you spoken to him again?"

Russell came and sat down on the edge of the bed. "Yes, this afternoon. He was disappointed. He can see that the sphere is attempting to communicate with us, but there is no machine in the world capable of deciphering it."

"I'm not as sensitive as you are to these attempts at communication, but do you really think that there's more to these headaches than just a warning of danger?"

"It's like with someone who doesn't speak French: even if you scream something at them in French they won't understand; they'll just get a headache."

"Then they should learn French," said Ellen sarcastically.

Russell got up, went over to the little bathroom and took a gulp of water from the faucet. Something about what she had just said lingered in his mind.

Learn French.

He thought about the test with the computer tomography and remembered how hard he had found it to meditate in the tube. When they had set it up in the sphere and he had been lying in it, he'd thought he'd heard Ellen's voice. What if that voice hadn't been in his head, but the sphere itself had been communicating with him? How did you know if the transporter was speaking to you? The machine activated something in your brain. If you looked at it like that, then the language of the sphere must feel like your own thoughts.

He couldn't stop thinking about it. He looked at his watch. Almost midnight. He got dressed and went to the door.

"Aren't you going to spend the night?" Ellen asked, disappointed. "Where are you going?"

"I'm going to learn French."

He left his bewildered girlfriend behind, grabbed a jacket from his room and made his way to the tunnel. The guards at the entrance looked at him askance, but let him pass despite the unusual hour.

All was quiet in the cave. The only light to be seen came from Gilbert's container. The physicist never seemed to knock off work.

Russell walked over to the black sphere, which had become the focus of his life over the last few weeks, and stepped inside. Immediately he felt a pressure in his head, but meanwhile he no longer found it painful.

Gilbert had put a table and chair next to the control pillar. Russell sat down and put his feet up on the table. Then he closed his eyes and tried a meditation exercise to suppress his thoughts.

Images and scraps of conversation drifted through his mind. Gently he pushed them aside, until he had reached a state of inner calm. But today images kept popping up in his consciousness without him being able to prevent it. He tried to grasp them, to understand them, but they were just fragments.

After a while he thought he could hear voices again—far-off voices. This time the voice resembled that of the general, although he couldn't understand what he was saying. More scenes passed through his mind. At one point he thought he could see a photo of the Milky Way, then an exotic landscape drifted in front of his eyes. He concentrated on the last mission, imagined the forest with the gigantic trees. The image turned into a video in his mind. He could see the dead bodies of the strange, headless creatures that he had killed in front of the sphere. Then he saw other creatures approaching; they leant over the dead animal and slowly dissolved it with their acid. The image was so realistic that Russell started. He realized that this film hadn't been created in his mind but had been planted in his mind from outside—as if he were watching a video transmission. In his head.

He opened his eyes. It was creepy. And yet he leaned over the control pillar and dialed a random code. In the next breath he closed his eyes. New scenes drifted into his mind. He saw an arid desert beneath a red sky. Tornados were swirling up dust and dancing over the rocky landscape. The image was so darn realistic and he knew if he were to go there with the transporter he would find this landscape. He felt it as clearly as never before. But at the same time he thought he could hear a voice deep inside him.

"Damn it, who are you?" he murmured.

I am me.

Russell started. The voice that had seemed so distant a moment ago was now loud and clear in his mind.

He opened his eyes. He had to convince himself that nobody was standing beside him, but nobody was there. So he took the video camera that was attached to the tripod beside him, turned it to face him and started recording.

Now he closed his eyes again.

"Who are you?" he asked.

I am me.

Russell repeated the words for the video camera.

"Are you the transporter?"

I am the transporter.

"Who am I?"

You are you.

Jesus, this is what it must feel like when you lost your mind!

"I'm Russell."

You are Russell.

"You know me?"

You have been on several transports.

"Where did I go on my last transport?"

He saw images of gigantic trees and dead, headless animals. At the same time the voice continued speaking.

Distance 12,455 light years. Gravity 0.96 times the value of here. Temperature currently 283 Kelvin ...

Russell was taken aback by the last piece of information.

"How do you know the units of measurement that I use for temperature? Why don't you say Celsius or Fahrenheit?"

I use the current definitions that I can read in your mind.

"You're reading my mind?"

I hear your thoughts.

"Who are you?"

I am the transporter. That is the definition you have given me.

It was too crazy.

"Where do you come from?"

I was built two astronomical units from here.

"Hang on a minute," he said and began to think

aloud. "Astronomical units indicate the distance from the Earth to the sun. That can't be. You were built in this solar system?"

I was built in this solar system.

"That's impossible! That doesn't make sense! Who built you?"

Images popped up in his inner eye. He saw an asteroid that slowly changed its shape. Other impressions floated through his mind. Suddenly it all made sense and he knew how the sphere had come to Earth.

Russell stood up and ran to the opening. He called over to Gilbert's container.

"Gilbert! Come out!"

After just a few seconds the surprised face of the physicist peered out of the door of the lab container.

"Gilbert! Get the general and the others. Quick!"

The physicist made a questioning gesture with his hands.

"The sphere is talking to me! And I can understand what it's saying!"

The scientist disappeared frantically into his container. Through the window Russell could see him on the phone.

He went back into the sphere and sat back down on the office chair. After a few seconds, Gilbert was standing beside him. The general and his friends arrived at the sphere ten minutes later.

Ellen leaned down to him. "What have you done?"

"I took a French lesson."

As her brow furrowed, he briefly explained how he had taken up contact with the sphere. Morrow shook his head in disbelief, but Russell concentrated again on the inner monologue that had surprisingly turned into a dialogue. He described the images that drifted across his inner eye.

"I see a small, metallic orb travelling through space. No more than about six feet wide. It arrives in the solar system and heads toward an asteroid. The orb dissolves. It consists of billions of tiny robots."

"Nanomachines," whispered Gilbert, fascinated.

"The microscopic robots start to reconstruct the asteroid. I can see how a bigger, black orb is growing out of the body of the asteroid. And another one. And another one. There are now twelve orbs sticking to the surface of this giant rock. They are transporter spheres. They detach themselves from the asteroid and fly toward different planets and moons in the solar system. One of them is the Earth. The sphere simply falls down into the water. And it remains there. For a long time. The Earth looks very different. The continents aren't where they are now. It must be millions of years ago. Other orbs are heading toward other planets. I can see Mars. Now a moon that's circling around Saturn. Now I can see the asteroid again. Two small metallic orbs are growing out of it. They accelerate in different directions. Damn it, the nanomachines built the transporter! With material from our asteroid belt. Then the nanomachines replicated themselves and flew on. In that way they brought transporters to every damn solar system in the galaxy. And it took millions of years."

Russell had a terrible headache. He stood up and left the sphere, but the pain didn't subside. He had overdone it.

The general sent him to bed to rest. He was to try and

make contact again the following day. The transports were suspended for the time being.

Albert had to support Russell as they left the cave. In the cool desert air in front of the tunnel he finally felt better.

"What does it feel like?" asked Albert.

"What do you mean?"

"I mean, how does it feel when that thing talks to you."

Russell sat down on the bench in front of the accommodation block. He didn't take the cigarette that Albert offered him.

"It's strange. A bit like being high on LSD. At first it's just thoughts that seem to be your own. But when you yield to them and concentrate on them, it's like a dam bursting. More and more images and voices pop up from nowhere—as if you were thinking somebody else's thoughts, but you still have the ability to control the direction they take. It's difficult to distinguish the images in your head from reality, they're so realistic. It's quite an effort. You have to simultaneously let go and concentrate. But I presume it will get easier over time. It's so strange and unfamiliar, almost frightening—as if you were losing control of yourself."

Ellen took his hand and brought him to his room. As he lay in bed he felt feverish, and the images that the sphere had shown him raced through his mind.

Despite the previous night's events, Russell felt okay again the following morning. The headache had disappeared and he was anxious to find out more. After breakfast, General Morrow and Gilbert brought him back down into the cave.

Before they entered the sphere again with the others, the general paused for a moment.

"When you establish contact with that thing again, please try and find out where the constructers come from and where we can find them. That is our most important goal."

They stepped into the sphere. Russell sat down in a comfy armchair that somebody had brought into the sphere, and closed his eyes.

It didn't take long until he was back in a trance-like state. Images raced around his mind. He could hear voices in the background, without being able to make out individual words. Russell focused on the first questions.

"Where do the spheres come from? Where do they originate?" he asked out loud.

Gilbert, who was standing next to him, hopped nervously from one foot to the other. Meanwhile Russell concentrated hard on the questions. This time a reaction came.

"I can see a film of the galaxy," he said. "In the film, the camera is zooming into the galaxy spiral, about half way between the center and the edge of the Milky Way. The camera is flying toward a single star."

"What's the symbol sequence for this star? The constructers must live there," said Gilbert in a flustered voice.

Russell saw the symbols in his inner eye. He stood up and went to the control pillar where he adjusted the code until it coincided with the image in his mind.

Gilbert couldn't hide his disappointment.

"That can't be. That's not a valid destination. A

field doesn't appear beneath the code."

"It is the right symbol sequence. But the sphere is telling me that it doesn't have any contact with the sphere registered there and that it can't call it."

"Perhaps these beings don't want any visitors. Perhaps they have made it impossible for external spheres to contact their home planet," said General Morrow.

"On how many planets do the builders of the spheres live? How far across the galaxy have they spread?" asked Gilbert.

Russell concentrated. Finally he said: "I'm not getting an answer to this question."

"On how many planets does life exist?" asked Gilbert.

"I can see another image of the Milky Way. Lots of the solar systems are highlighted in color. I would say every tenth system is colored."

"Oh my God!"

"On how many of them is there intelligent life?" probed Gilbert, and Russell concentrated on the question.

"The colors are disappearing," he explained. "Only one point in the Milky Way is still colored. The camera is zooming in on it. It's Earth."

"That can't be!" spluttered Gilbert in a shocked voice. "We can't be the only civilization in the Milky Way!"

"What about the home system of the builders? And the systems that surround them? They must have colonized those."

Russell looked again at the mental image, but had to give a negative answer: "I can't see anything highlighted."

Everyone was silent as they digested this information. If they were to believe what the sphere was telling them, there were no intelligent alien beings in the galaxy.

"What else does the sphere have to say? Who were these alien builders?" asked Albert.

"I'm not getting an answer. I presume that the sphere's intelligence is limited. However, I do have access to a map of the Milky Way and all the spheres. I can ask for images and about the environmental conditions."

"If we can't select the home system of the builders, how can we find out what happened?" asked Morrow.

"See if you can find out which system is closest to the constructers'. If there are any clues to be found, then probably in their immediate vicinity," urged the physicist.

"Yes, I can see a neighboring system," said Russell. "The camera is moving into this system. It consists of Jupiter-like gaseous planets and an Earth-like world. It is covered completely in ice. I have an image from the sphere in my head. I presume it is a kind of live transmission. The camera is swiveling around. Hey, there's a building!"

"What kind of building?" asked Ellen.

"It looks like a warehouse. Rectangular shape. Not very high. It's hard to judge the exact dimensions since I don't have anything to compare it with. Perhaps three-hundred feet long, but I can't say for sure. It's completely black. Like the transporter. I can't see any windows or doors."

"Any activity?" asked General Morrow.

"No. The building is all alone and deserted in the

landscape."

The general stood up and turned to Holbrook, who was standing beside him. "Prepare an expedition. That's where we'll go. Tomorrow morning. Finally we're going to find some answers."

"Who's going?"

"You're in command, Holbrook. And Harris, Bridgeman, Slayton, Hilmers and Rogers will come too."

"I would like to go this time," said Gilbert.

Morrow snorted with irritation. "Do we have to discuss this again? You're staying here. That's my final word. Harris, what are the environmental conditions on this planet? Do we need space suits?"

"The atmosphere is breathable. But it's cold. Very cold. Minus twenty-two degrees Fahrenheit. Like in the Antarctic."

"Right. I'll get us some winter uniforms. We start tomorrow at 0900 hours."

34. Origins

The group stood in their white uniforms in the sphere. They carried only light backpacks, but were armed. Russell realized that he could give the transporter instructions with his thoughts. He simply told the sphere which destination to select, and then ordered the transport to start.

This time they were travelling to the alleged colony of the sphere constructers on the ice planet. When they arrived, Russell could immediately feel the cold air. At the same time, he realized that he could communicate with the sphere on this planet just as he could with the one on Earth. They were obviously connected to one another. It didn't make any difference whatsoever to which sphere he spoke.

"Let's go!" said Holbrook and opened the inner sphere.

"Oh!" gasped Ellen.

There was equipment lying around everywhere. It was the first time that they had found something in another sphere. Black metal stairs led down from the transporter. Russell walked down them. The steps were a little too low and narrow for humans. But the railing was too high. And yet: the aliens seemed to have a similar physiology. The equipment lying around the sphere looked strange, but had familiar control elements: switches, push-buttons, dials. What did it tell them about these aliens? That they must have fingers? Or could dials also be turned with tentacles?

"Don't touch anything, is that clear?" ordered Holbrook.

Russell looked more closely at the surfaces of the

objects. The strange pieces of machinery were covered in a fine layer of dust.

"When was this transporter last used?" he murmured. The answer came almost immediately. Almost 270 million years ago.

Holy shit. It was a miracle that the equipment hadn't even rusted. Build for eternity. They could do that.

"We'll go outside and head for the building," said Holbrook and made an opening in the sphere.

They ventured out into the strange world. An icy wind tousled Russell's hair. He pulled up his hood and buried his neck deep in his collar. Snow crystals spattered against his face and immediately his eyes started to water. Not even the goggles helped.

All around them, the ground was covered in snow. You couldn't see far, everything further away than several hundred feet was lost in a hazy mist. In front of them, Russell could just about make out the strange building that he had seen in his inner eye. It was black and looked like an elongated shoebox, three-hundred feet long and thirty feet high. There were no windows to be seen. He trudged over together with the rest of the group.

"I can't find an entrance!" shouted Vance Hilmers into the storm. "The walls are totally smooth. Looks like a giant monolith."

Holbrook was the first to get to the building. He placed the flat of his hand on the wall. An opening appeared like with the transporters. They stepped inside.

The building appeared to consist of just one enormous room. There was hardly any furniture. Russell shook his head. He had expected something different.

"There's something over there." Ellen pointed at the opposite end of the hall. As they got closer, Russell could make out a control panel. It reminded him of the control pillar in the transporter, but this one was much bigger. There was a kind of chair next to it, which was also covered in a fine layer of dust. Hilmers wanted to sit down on it, but Holbrook held him back.

"Don't," he said and held him firmly by the arm.

"What's the problem?" Hilmers looked at Holbrook in confusion.

"Just that there's dust on the chair, and nowhere else."

"Yeah, and?"

"It's been a hell of a long time since anything happened here. If somebody died here, even his skeleton would have turned to dust by now."

Hilmers' eyes widened. "You mean that ..."

"... somebody died on that chair? Yes, that's what I mean."

Russell gulped. Was that all that was left of the aliens? Dust? The building looked so unfinished—as if someone had built an empty warehouse and then just left it standing in the landscape.

What on earth happened here?

He had a feeling the answer would shock him.

Holbrook ran his fingers over the black console, but nothing happened.

"Do you feel anything?" asked Holbrook.

"No," said Russell. "There's nothing here. No attempts at communication. Sorry."

"Spread yourselves out! See if you can find anything."

"There's something lying on the ground," said

Ellen. "What is it?"

Russell came closer.

It looks like a dice. It's even about the same size. Completely black.

"What could it be?"

"No idea. Take it."

Ellen slipped the thing into her jacket pocket, then they searched the hall together, square foot by square foot, but there was nothing more to be found.

"There's no point in staying any longer," said Holbrook. "We'll turn back. General Morrow has to organize a systematic reconnaissance mission." He looked around the room one last time and murmured a few words: "Strange. Really strange."

They left the building and, feeling resigned, trudged back through the icy storm to the transporter before returning to Earth.

35. Answers

General Morrow was waiting for them in the outer sphere. Holbrook reported back. Morrow looked disappointed.

"You really didn't find anything?"

"Only this," said Ellen and took the little cube out of her pocket.

"What could it be?" murmured Russell. To his surprise he immediately got an answer.

A data carrier.

"A data carrier?"

He had asked the question out loud. Everyone looked at him.

A data carrier.

"How do you read it?"

I have access, and therefore you have access.

"I have access?" asked Russell in surprise.

"What's on it?"

Images appeared before his eyes. The voice in his head provided him with explanations. Russell described what he could see and hear to the others.

"I can see the ice planet. Someone is sitting on the chair by the console. Jesus, it's an alien! He has a similar build to a human but looks completely strange. His skin looks like black leather. He has a small head attached to his torso. No neck. I can't see eyes, mouth or a nose. He has two thin legs and two thin arms with delicate fingers. He doesn't seem to be wearing any clothing. He's sitting silently in his chair in front of the console and is recording his thoughts on the data carrier. The image is getting blurry. Damn it, that was incredible! I can hear what the alien is thinking. Unbelievable. But he's scared. I can sense his despair.

Deep despair. Now I can see the inside of another building. It must be on the alien's home planet. There are rows of black spheres. I get it. It's a research facility. That's where they developed the sphere technology. They've just started to establish their transport network. A few years earlier they sent the first orb to the neighboring star with nanomachines. They are celebrating the fact that the first sphere has gone into operation in another solar system. Apparently this is the only way they found of conducting interstellar space travel. That's why they sent off the transporter factories, and that's how they wanted to populate the galaxy in the long term. They wanted to establish their first colony on the ice planet. The alien who made the recording on the data carrier was responsible for setting up base. Later it was to become a research station. The alien built the assembly hall with the help of nanomachines and then returned to his home planet. When he arrived all hell had broken loose. Something had happened; something had gone wrong with a new research project. I don't understand exactly, but they had created a black hole in their laboratory. A small black hole, no bigger than an atom. Gravity had pulled it into the interior of their planet and it was now orbiting around the center of their world. On its way it sucked up matter and finally came to a stop at the planetary core. It grew and grew, as it slowly devoured their planet. The image I can see is horrific. Their once blue planet shrunk into itself. In the final phase of destruction, huge tidal waves, miles high, swept over the surface of the planet. In the end, entire continental plates slipped over each other, while the planet collapsed in free fall into the black hole at its heart.

The alien was just able to save himself from the apocalypse by transporting himself back to the base in the neighboring solar system. He was stranded there. The last survivor of a proud, technologically advanced civilization. I'm reading his thoughts, which he recorded on the cube. The alien's feelings are indescribable. Their civilization had conquered hunger. There were no diseases anymore, no wars. They were well on their way to creating a utopia. Nobody needed to work. Automated factories could create everything that the aliens needed or wanted. It was a world of plenty, but at the same time they had found a way of not burdening their environment. Thanks to science and technology they had left all negatives behind them. But in the end, their thirst for knowledge destroyed them."

"Shocking!" whispered Holbrook, but Russell continued.

"The alien was stuck on the ice planet. He knew that he would die. There was no food on this planet. But there was nowhere else for him to go. There were only two planets with transporters, and one of them had been destroyed. The alien recorded his thoughts on the data carrier. He hoped that at some point in the distant future other beings would find a way of using the transporters and discover the story of the civilization that gave the galaxy this transport system. Then he sat down in his chair and waited to die."

"Incredible," said Gilbert.

"They destroyed themselves, but their legacy lives on. Their transporter factories flew from solar system to solar system. They dropped the black spheres everywhere, replicated themselves, and travelled on to the next solar system. It must have taken millions of years. The aliens themselves never got to experience it. We are obviously the only intelligent race to have developed after them. And thanks to their transporter, the whole galaxy is now at our disposal."

"But we still don't understand the technology," General Morrow said crossly. "Our goal was to find out how these things work. And we haven't managed that."

"Don't worry," said Russell. "Their entire knowledge is saved in the spheres. I have full access to it."

"What?" cried Gilbert in surprise.

"Yes, I only need to think of a question and the answer will appear. If I don't understand something I can get further information. When I ask myself how the transporters work, diagrams, formula and production techniques appear before my eyes." He stopped talking. As he spoke, he got an uneasy feeling.

"But only you can talk with the sphere," complained the physicist. "It needs to be scientists and engineers who have access to this knowledge."

"You're wrong. Anyone can communicate with the sphere. I just learnt it quicker because I used to meditate. You need to separate your own thoughts from those that are planted in your head. The simplest way is just not to think anymore. It's like in our own language: in order to listen, you first have to stop talking. Once you've mastered that, the rest will follow automatically."

Gilbert shrugged doubtfully. "You mean I will be able to talk with the sphere? And ask it everything it knows?"

"It could take a while, but yes.'"

The physicist's gazed around the room as he absorbed this information. He had achieved his goal. He would acquire knowledge that no human before him had had.

Russell glanced over at Morrow, who was gazing into the distance, lost in thought. The general, too, had attained his goal. He would no longer be a laughing stock. And yet Russell felt uneasy at the thought that the knowledge of these aliens would soon be completely at the disposal of human beings.

"What were the aliens working on?" asked Gilbert. "What led to their downfall? We need to avoid ever falling into the same trap."

"I didn't really understand it," replied Russell. "Apparently the teleportation system required little wormholes to be temporarily increased in size for the transport. At some point they had the idea of creating one giant, stable wormhole. To do this they ..." He tried to understand the film that was playing in his head. The sphere reacted to his wish and new images appeared which clarified what he hadn't been able to understand. "They amplified gravitational waves," he explained. "Or did they bring them into resonance? Is that the right word? I don't know. In any case they created a black hole without any mass, purely with these gravitational waves. It should have collapsed, but it didn't. It grew. Do you understand what I'm saying, Gilbert?"

The physicist nodded slowly. "Yes, Russell, I understand. The technology that they had at their disposal must have been incredible. They could create defects in spacetime and even black holes without matter. They created a stable black hole that couldn't collapse due to Hawking radiation. That was their downfall. They should have created a rotating, electrically charged black hole. That could have been magnetically controlled. Oh God, the potential would have been limitless. Just think of the possibilities of energy generation!" The physicist tripped over his words in excitement.

"Doctor, you need to keep your hands off this," warned Russell. "The aliens wiped themselves out with their knowledge."

"We'll be more careful. We will take all necessary precautions."

"The aliens were thousands of years ahead of us. And even they were unable to avoid the catastrophe. What makes you think you could do it better?" Russell's concern was growing in proportion to Gilbert's excitement.

"We'll be as careful as we can be!" he promised. "But we can't let this knowledge go to waste. A stable black hole, magnetically secured in a research facility. The possibilities are endless!"

Russell saw something light up in Gilbert's eyes, and he realized that genius always went hand in hand with madness.

The colonel didn't seem too impressed either.

"General," said Holbrook soberly. "If we put this technology into the hands of the scientists, we will destroy ourselves the way the aliens did."

But General Morrow responded with a determined expression. "That's what Oppenheimer said after inventing the atomic bomb. Be realistic. It's our duty to make this technology available to our country and it is the duty of our politicians to make sure it is used responsibly."

Russell thought of President Bigby, who was sure to launch a comprehensive research program to develop weapons using this new technology. Soon several countries would be threatening each other with the destruction of the world. He thought about "mad scientists", like Gilbert, who would work on developing machines that would be capable of extinguishing the entire human race if just the slightest mistake was made. In his mind's eye, he again saw the alien's planet collapsing in on itself and it dawned on him that he was seeing the future of the Earth.

"It mustn't happen," whispered Ellen in his ear.

Russell could feel a lump in his throat.

My God, what can I do?

He looked at the general, who was staring at him coldly. Then he noticed the silver chain around the general's neck. Then he looked over to Gilbert, who was wearing the same chain around his neck.

"Would a nuclear explosion destroy the sphere?" he murmured quietly, so that nobody could hear. The answer came immediately.

Yes, if the sphere is open.

Russell looked at Ellen and winked at her. She winked back, barely noticeably. Next he looked over to Albert. Bridgeman returned his glance and nodded.

Russell's fist shot forward and landed on the general's chest. He fell to the ground with a groan. Russell jumped forward and ripped the chain with the key from the general's throat.

Gilbert went pale. The scientist knew what he was planning and ran to the entrance of the sphere. Holbrook pulled him back.

Russell took the general's pistol. Morrow was still doubled up on the floor, groaning. Then he went over to the physicist and ripped the chain from his neck.

"You wouldn't dare, Harris! You can't be that crazy!" cried Gilbert, struggling to escape Albert's grasp.

"I'm starting to ask myself which of us is the crazy one," said Russell and ran off. The others followed him. Vance Hilmers also followed the group uncertainly. He hadn't grasped what was going on. Jim was surprised, too, but had quickly caught on.

"Quick, to Gilbert's lab container!"

They ran through the opening to the laboratory.

Behind them, General Morrow appeared in the opening of the sphere. He supported himself on the wall of the sphere and screamed in the direction of the guards at the tunnel entrance.

"Shoot them! Stop them at all costs!"

The soldiers looked incredulously at the general. As if in slow motion, one of them drew his pistol.

"Shoot! They mustn't reach the container," thundered Morrow.

Russell raised his own pistol and shot over the soldiers' heads. He didn't want to hit them, but hoped it would make them run for cover. The soldiers ducked behind a crate and fired, but Russell had already reached the container. Ellen and Jim followed him. Albert closed the door.

"Where's Hilmers?" cried Ellen.

"Dead. Hit in the head by a bullet," Albert replied.

Russell went over to the panel with which the nuclear bomb beneath their feet could be activated. Outside they could here the booming voice of the general.

"Harris! Don't do it! Come out immediately, that's an order!"

"Do it," countered Ellen. "This is the only right thing to do." She placed a hand on his shoulder.

Russell inserted the first key and turned it. A red light glimmered on the console. He inserted the second key.

"How long?" asked Jim.

"Half an hour," answered Russell.

"Now turn the key!" urged Holbrook.

Russell turned the key. Outside they could hear the howling of the alarm sirens.

Gilbert was bellowing with anger.

Russell looked out of the window. Engineers and soldiers were storming to the exit of the tunnel. Gilbert was babbling to the general.

"We have to dig it up!"

"Forget it, that would take hours," said the general bitterly.

Gilbert hurried over to a hatch in the floor and opened it.

The general indicated to the guard. The soldier grabbed the physicist from behind and dragged him to the entrance of the tunnel. Gilbert struggled and shouted, but he didn't stand a chance against the brawny soldiers.

Slowly General Morrow walked over to the container.

"Harris! You've made your decision and you'll pay for it. You will go down with the transporter."

The general turned on his heel and marched to the tunnel entrance. He was the last to leave the tunnel. The heavy steel door to the tunnel closed. A short time later they heard a dull rumble. The ground was shaking.

"They've blown up the tunnel. We're trapped," said Albert.

"We're going to die," gasped Jim.

"No," replied Russell. "We're going to go with the transporter to the forest planet. We still have 25 minutes. Grab every bit of equipment that you can find and take it to the transporter. Go!"

Jim and Albert ran to the weapons depot and threw hand grenades, pistols and anything that seemed useful into a big crate. They dragged this to the conveyor belt next to the transporter. Meanwhile, Ellen got food and medication from the storage container and Russell threw all the space suits as well as other pieces of equipment into a crate. Soon the inside of the transporter was piled high with crates.

"How much time have we got left?" asked Jim breathlessly, as he unloaded another container into the sphere.

"Ten minutes. At five minutes I'll call you over to the transporter. Keep going! Grab everything you possibly can!"

Russell also looked for more things. He ran to the container where the weapons were kept. Meanwhile Albert took a big crate from a shelf and opened it.

"What's that?" he asked and pointed at several basketball-sized metallic balls.

Russell went over. "Those are atomic bombs. Small loads for tactical missions. Take them."

Now he hurried over to Jim, who helped him drag an electrical generator into the sphere. Ellen was hauling the fifth can of gasoline to the sphere.

Russell looked at his watch. "Okay. Five more minutes. Everyone in the sphere! Come on, Albert, quick!"

Gasping, Bridgeman dragged two heavy toolboxes into the transporter. "I'm ready."

"One more minute. Is the entrance to the outer sphere open?"

"Yes."

"Good. Then the transporter will be destroyed together with the cave."

Russell thought about the forest planet and immediately got a response from the sphere that the destination had been set.

"Start the transport," he commanded.

They had arrived. They had landed in an alien world.

Once they had gotten the equipment onto the ground in the outer sphere with the help of the conveyor belt, Russell went over to the control column. He tapped in the symbol for Earth. The field for starting the transport no longer appeared. The transporter on Earth had been destroyed.

He opened the outer skin and stepped outside. The others followed him. There was no sign of the acid-secreting animals. The body that they had left behind on their last mission had also disappeared. Everything seemed very quiet. They couldn't hear a single sound.

"And now what?" asked Jim.

"We'll make ourselves at home," said Russell. "We'll block off a large area around the sphere with electric fences, mines and barbwire. The fences should keep the creatures at bay. To begin with we can sleep in the sphere, then we'll see how it goes."

"I looked through the crates with the food," said Ellen. "We've got enough to last us a few months. By then we need to have found something edible."

"We've got two radioisotope generators, each with an output of five kilowatts," added Albert. "So we don't need to worry about electricity for the time being."

"It all went so quickly. I haven't event really understood yet what happened. Was that really necessary?" asked Jim.

"You saw the physicist," said Russell. "He would have done anything to create a black hole in his lab. Without giving a damn about the risk. The aliens were far more advanced then us and even they weren't able to control their own technology. It was only a matter of time and our world would have been destroyed too. Humans aren't mature enough for technology like that. And I doubt they ever will be. The only chance was to take the sphere away from them."

"And now we're stuck in the back of beyond, without a possibility of returning," responded Albert bitterly.

"The whole galaxy is at our disposal," said Russell. "We can go anywhere we want."

"Just not back to Earth."

They were silent for a while, each of them lost in thought. Finally Ellen cleared her throat.

"There will be a new space race," she prophesized.

"What? What do you mean?" asked Jim,

"There are other transporters in the solar system. Including on Mars. Russell said so himself. There will be a space race between the nations on Earth to get their hands on the spheres. And then they'll play around with the technology again. We've only given the Earth some breathing space."

"It could take a long time until they find another transporter."

Ellen laughed. "It'll go quicker than you think. For years now, they've been mapping Mars in high resolution using research satellites. It's possible that the sphere is already visible on one of the images but until now they thought it was something else. I guarantee you: in ten years at the latest there will be a manned station on Mars right next to a transporter."

"We can't do anything about that," said Russell. "We have to take care of ourselves for now."

"What are we going to do here?" asked Jim glumly. "We make ourselves at home and perhaps we even manage to survive. We've got enough stuff. And then? Will we watch each grow old? What kind of future is that?"

Russell sat down in the grass and leant against one of the tree trunks. Suddenly he felt very tired. He tried come up with an answer, but couldn't think of one.

36. Epilogue

"Are you ready?" asked Russell.

"Yes, I'm ready. Let's go," said Holbrook.

Russell checked the displays on his space suit one last time and started the transport.

As the gravity became abruptly weaker, he could feel his stomach lurching. He looked at the scanner in his right hand.

"Gravity 0.38 g," he said. "Pressure six times ten to the minus three. Mostly carbon dioxide. Some nitrogen and oxygen. Temperature fourteen degrees Fahrenheit."

"Sounds good," said his companion. "We've arrived. Let's go outside."

They created an opening into the outer sphere and lowered themselves on a rope. Russell opened his bag and took out the soccer-ball-sized nuclear explosive device. He put it on the floor of the sphere, and set the detonator for one hour.

No need to hurry.

"Shall we have a look outside?" asked Holbrook.

"Sure, lets."

Russell went to the outer wall, and laid his hand on the skin. A red light flooded into the opening.

"After you," said Holbrook.

Russell stepped outside. He almost got his foot caught on the edge of the opening and stumbled outside faster than he wanted.

"Shit," he swore.

"Now, now. Considering you're the first person to set foot on Mars, you could have said a few more dignified words!" joked Holbrook.

"Nobody'll hear them anyway," he countered.

Russell gazed over the barren, rugged landscape: just red red boulders and sand as far as the eye could see. In the distance, a mountain range of brownish cliffs was silhouetted against the horizon. The sky was clear and of a reddish color with a slight tinge of green.

"Jesus, it's bleak here. Can't understand why you astronauts were so desperate to go to Mars."

"You should see the moon. That's even bleaker."

"Let's go and finish this job off." Russell turned around and wanted to return to the sphere, but Holbrook grabbed his arm.

"Wait. Look at that." The astronaut pointed at a bright point in the sky. It sparkled in a bluish light.

"Is that what I think it is?" asked Russell.

"Yes, that's Earth."

Russell looked up at the blue point and felt a lump forming in his throat. Five years had passed since they had fled from Earth with the transporter. They had settled on Avalon and found ways of surviving. But he had never been able to forget that there were other spheres in the solar system that would be found at some point. So they had dug out the tactical nuclear weapons. First they had destroyed the transporter on the Saturn moon Titan, then the one on Enceladus. This was followed by the spheres on Vesta, Europa, Oberon, Mercury and Sedna. They couldn't get to the sphere on Venus. The outside pressure would have squashed them to pulp in their space suits. But humans on Earth wouldn't be able to get there for the time being, either. Albert had an idea of how to send an atomic bomb to Venus in the transporter, but he didn't want to talk about it and grumbled over his calculations. That just left the transporter on Mars. And that was on the agenda for today.

Russell couldn't take his eyes of the bright speck. There was something mystical about the way it shimmered blue.

"How far away is Earth?" he asked.

"The distance from the sun is about thirty degrees. I would guess around a hundred-and-twenty-million miles."

I will never be this close to Earth again. All the people I knew, loved, and hated. All the places I've ever been. All of them condensed into one tiny speck.

The last time he'd been on Earth was five years ago. He wondered what had happened there in the meantime.

The sphere on Mars lay in an exposed area. With the detailed satellite images of our Mars probes, it had probably already been discovered. Were spaceships already being built or on their way here?

He tore himself away and climbed into the transporter. Holbrook followed him. They left the outer sphere open.

Russell went over to the atomic bomb that lay beneath the sphere and activated it. The countdown had begun. In an hour there would be no more transporters in reach of humanity. Humans would have to take the more laborious path of developing technologies by themselves. It would take thousands of years before they had the technology to build a transporter. Russell hoped that technical and scientific know-how was not the only thing that became more advanced.

Without exchanging a word they climbed back into the transporter and returned to Avalon. Ellen had chosen the name for their new home. Russell wasn't familiar with the Arthurian legend, and she had only briefly summarized it for him. But the name had something mystical about it, that's why he had agreed to it.

He and Holbrook took off their space suits and left the sphere. A little boy ran toward Russell with outstretched arms.

"Hello Jim? What are you up to?"

"Hello Papa. Are you back?"

"Yes I'm back."

"Will you stay here now?"

"Yes, Jim. Papa isn't going away again."

"Good."

Jim ran off. He picked up a stick from the ground and ran to his sister who was playing with a friend. Holbrook had disappeared into his house.

The wood from the mammoth trees made good building material. With the equipment they had brought with them, it hadn't been difficult to build little wooden houses for the colony. The first winter had been hard. They had rationed their food and had to constantly defend themselves against attacks from the headless beasts. But after a year, things had improved. They had found edible plants and a way of defending themselves against the creatures: They discovered that they communicated by means of ultrasound. So Holbrook had created a transmitter that drove the beasts crazy. Now they hardly saw them anymore. They stayed well clear of the camp.

During this time, Russell and Ellen had gone with the transporter to the grass planet and the Summers planetoid to speak to the scientists and soldiers. The men and women had all been far from pleased when they discovered that they couldn't return to Earth. Many of them had families that they would never see again. There had been a lot of bad blood, but many had also shown understanding for the decision to destroy the transporter. In the end they had come to terms with the situation and had come to Avalon to help establish the camp.

Then Ellen had become pregnant. They had wanted to name their son Kyle, but a few days before the birth, Jim Rogers had died of a fever and they had named their newborn after him. Meanwhile, Jim had a sister and in a month another brother would be born. It hadn't been planned. They hadn't intended to establish a colony; the children had come of their own accord. But a few months ago they had talked about the long-term prospects of their settlement. They wanted a future for their children. There were now forty-two adults living here: twenty women and twenty-two men. Ellen worked out that the genetic diversity was sufficient for the colony to survive. On Earth there were also examples of small populations that had survived and proliferated. Russell hoped the plan would work. It would be terrible for one of the children to one day be the last living human on this planet. But his initial skepticism had transformed into hope.

He walked through the little settlement and saw Albert working in a forge next to his house. He had discovered iron ore nearby and immediately immersed himself in making tools. Russell had gone on several long explorations and had discovered bitumen in a swamp. In summer they wanted to set up a camp there and mine for oil. Holbrook had already drawn up plans for a makeshift refinery.

We have everything we need to survive, and the children have a real chance.

Russell opened the door to their house. The fire in the grate provided cozy warmth. He took off his windbreaker and hung it on a hook on the wall.

Ellen sat in an armchair that he had built and covered with the leather of one of the headless animals. She was asleep. Her face was completely relaxed. Her hand rested protectively on her stomach, where little Jake was growing.

Russell kissed her gently on the forehead and whispered softly into her ear: "I'm home."

END

More books by Phillip P. Peterson coming 2017:
Transport 2: Death Flood
Transport 3: Death Zone
Paradox - Eon Abyss

For updates and notifications about new releases feel free to sign in to the newsletter:
http://eepurl.com/cmCVWn

For updates, questions and new releases you can also find the author at Facebook:
https://www.facebook.com/PetersonAuthor-206656313081747
or search there for "PetersonAuthor"

Twitter:
https://twitter.com/PetersonAuthor

TRANSPORT
by Phillip P. Peterson

Cover with material from FOTOLIA.com:
Image "Astronaut in the tunnels" by I. Kovalenko

Contact:
contact@petersonauthor.com

Made in the USA
San Bernardino, CA
27 November 2016